Kate Fortune's Journal Entry

If there is one thing a Fortune man knows from the moment he's born, it's how to woo a lady. And my Riley seems to be no exception. Ever since Angelica Dodd refused his marriage proposal, Riley has sent her enough roses in the past week to build a float for the Rose Parade. And then there are the diamond earrings, bracelet and emerald pendant.... Seems as if courtship was less expensive in my day. But then I've heard it on good authority that Riley and Angelica are way past the courtship stage. And even if Riley is now proposing for the sake of their unborn child, I saw the way he looked at Angelica at her brother's funeral. And the way she clung to him. Once Angelica overcomes her foolish pride, this is a marriage that will last forever!

Dear Reader,

Our 20th anniversary pledge to you, our devoted readers, is a promise to continue delivering passionate, powerful, provocative love stories from your favorite Silhouette Desire authors for all the years to come!

As an anniversary treat, we've got a special book for you from the incomparable Annette Broadrick. *Marriage Prey* is a romance between the offspring of two couples from Annette's earliest Desire books, which Silhouette reissued along with a third early Desire novel last month as *Maximum Marriage: Men on a Mission*. Bestselling author Mary Lynn Baxter brings you November's MAN OF THE MONTH...*Her Perfect Man*. A minister and a reformed party girl fall for each other in this classic opposites-attract love story. *A Cowboy's Gift* is the latest offering by RITA Award winner Anne McAllister in her popular CODE OF THE WEST miniseries.

Another RITA winner, Caroline Cross, delivers the next installment of the exciting Desire miniseries FORTUNE'S CHILDREN: THE GROOMS with *Husband—or Enemy?* Dixie Browning's miniseries THE PASSIONATE POWERS continues with *The Virgin and the Vengeful Groom*, part of our extra-sensual BODY & SOUL promotion. And Sheri WhiteFeather has created another appealing Native American hero in *Night Wind's Woman*.

So please join us in celebrating twenty glorious years of category romance by indulging yourself with all six of these compelling love stories from Silhouette Desire!

Enjoy!

Joan Marlow Golan

Joan Marlow Golan
Senior Editor, Silhouette Desire

Please address questions and book requests to:
Silhouette Reader Service
U.S.: 3010 Walden Ave., P.O. Box 1325, Buffalo, NY 14269
Canadian: P.O. Box 609, Fort Erie, Ont. L2A 5X3

Husband—or Enemy?

CAROLINE CROSS

Published by Silhouette Books

America's Publisher of Contemporary Romance

Special thanks and acknowledgment are given to
Caroline Cross for her contribution to the
Fortune's Children: The Grooms series.

This book is dedicated with much appreciation to my
wonderful brainstorming partner, Susan Andersen,
for holding my hand and keeping me on track.
And to Ann Leslie Tuttle.

 SILHOUETTE BOOKS

ISBN 0-373-76330-1

HUSBAND—OR ENEMY?

Books by Caroline Cross

Silhouette Desire

Dangerous #810
Rafferty's Angel #851
Truth or Dare #910
Operation Mommy #939
Gavin's Child #1013
The Baby Blizzard #1079
The Notorious Groom #1143
The Paternity Factor #1173
Cinderella's Tycoon #1238
The Rancher and the Nanny #1298
Husband—or Enemy? #1330

CAROLINE CROSS

always loved to read, but it wasn't until she discovered romance that she felt compelled to write, fascinated by the chance to explore the positive power of love in people's lives. She grew up in Yakima, Washington, the "Apple Capital of the World," attended the University of Puget Sound and now lives outside Seattle, where she (tries to) work at home despite the chaos created by two telephone-addicted teenage daughters and a husband with a fondness for home improvement projects. Pleased to have recently been #1 on a national bestseller list, she was thrilled to win the 1999 Romance Writers of America's RITA Award for Best Short Contemporary Novel and to have been called "one of the best" writers of romance today by *Romantic Times Magazine*. Caroline believes in writing from the heart—and having a good brainstorming partner. She loves hearing from readers and can be reached at P.O. Box 47375, Seattle, Washington 98146. Please include a SASE for reply.

F⊙RTUNE'S
Children

Meet the Arizona Fortunes—a family with a legacy of wealth, influence and power. As they gather for a host of weddings, a shocking plot against the family is revealed...and passionate new romances are ignited.

RILEY FORTUNE: Nobody had ever mistaken him for a saint. But he certainly wasn't guilty of murdering Angelica's brother!

ANGELICA DODD: How dare Riley Fortune think he could just waltz back into her life after a three-month absence, crook a finger and believe that she'd do anything he wanted? Especially when he wanted her to marry him for the sake of their unborn child!

MIKE DODD: Angelica knew that trouble had always seemed to follow her little brother. And she also knew that the only crime Riley was guilty of was offering her a caring shoulder when she'd needed it most.

One

Riley Fortune narrowed his pale gray eyes against the shifting nighttime shadows and glanced at his thin gold wristwatch.

The luminous dial read 10:45.

With a faint sigh, he propped his hips against the gleaming fender of his silver Corvette, crossed his legs at the ankle and settled in to wait.

Overhead, the moon gleamed like an oversize pearl in the star-strewn sky. Closer to earth, a flirtatious May breeze threaded the warm Arizona night, ruffling his thick black hair and tugging playfully at his white silk shirt and pale linen slacks.

Riley paid no attention, his focus instead on the service entrance of the Camel Corral Steakhouse some forty feet away. Minutes ticked past, trying his already thin reserve of patience. Finally, the door opened. Amidst a burst of feminine chatter, a trio of waitresses walked out, all identically dressed in black slacks, white tuxedo shirts and black bow ties.

He started to straighten, only to fall back as he realized that none of them was the woman he wanted.

He felt a surge of annoyance, which he did his best to shrug away. After all, what did he expect? That after three months of avoiding Angelica Dodd he could suddenly decide he wanted to see her and she'd instantly appear?

Well…yeah. The realization sent a faint smile— his first in more days than he could remember— curving across his brooding mouth. All right. So he was accustomed to women chasing after him, then dropping at his feet like so many overripe plums with hardly more than a snap of his fingers. So what?

So you know damn well Angelica's not like that. The only reason she succumbed to your charms, considerable though they may be, is because she was hurting—and because you took advantage of her. Although even for you, seducing a woman only hours after her brother's funeral has to be a new low.

But then, nobody had ever mistaken him for a saint. A fact that had been forcefully driven home a week ago when he'd gone from being merely a suspect to actually being charged with that same brother's murder.

He tensed at the thought of what had happened to

Mike Dodd—and at the remembered humiliation of his own arrest, of being escorted out of Fortune Construction headquarters in handcuffs and hauled into the Pueblo police station to be booked and have his fingerprints and mugshot taken. Nor was he likely to forget the stricken look that had been on his mother's face when he'd been brought before the judge for arraignment. He'd never forgive himself for being the cause.

But that was a subject for another day, he reminded himself sharply, rolling his shoulders in an attempt to relieve their knotted tension. Tonight's little drama involved an entirely different kind of life-altering situation...

Across the way, the restaurant door opened again and another waitress exited. And though this one was dressed exactly the way the others had been, Riley recognized her immediately.

Angelica. He came to attention, watching intently as she came to a stop as the heavy door swung shut behind her. Blissfully unaware of his scrutiny, she yanked off her apron, tugged her hair clip loose and gave her head a shake. He knew it had to be his imagination, but he could have sworn he heard her sigh of pleasure as the shiny mass of her hair tumbled around her shoulders the instant before she resumed her trek across the parking lot.

A sudden heaviness filled Riley's groin as a vision flashed through his mind. A vision of her naked, her skin like satin, all that pale, silvery brown hair fanned out across her pristine white sheets, her leaf-green eyes locked on his as he slowly thrust himself inside her—

He sucked in a breath. *Damn.* Why couldn't he quit thinking about that night? Why, after all this time did it keep sneaking up on him, ambushing him at the least opportune times? And why did his recollections have to be so vivid, to the point where he knew all he had to do was shut his eyes and he'd be able to feel her, smell her, taste her?

With an oath, he pushed himself away from the Corvette, unable to stay still a second longer.

His abrupt movement drew his quarry's eye. She jerked to a stop and a kaleidoscope of emotion—surprise, uncertainty, welcome, wariness—flashed across her vivid face. "Riley?"

"Hello, Angelica."

She took a moment before she answered, slowly drawing an air of indifference around her like a cloak. "Well, gosh. What are you doing here? That fancy car of yours run out of gas?"

"We need to talk."

"We do, huh? About what?"

He opened his mouth with every intention of telling her. After all, he'd been thinking about nothing else for hours, ever since he'd overheard a pair of clerks at Baker's Pharmacy avidly gossiping about him and Mike, the Dodd family's less-than-stellar history—and Angelica's recent purchases of a home pregnancy test and prescription prenatal vitamins.

Under different circumstances, he might have shrugged that last bit off as nothing more than a bit of malicious slander. But there was no way he could forget that—for the first time ever—he'd failed to use protection the night they'd spent together. Or that she'd reportedly fainted on the job last week.

Taken all together it had made a kind of sense that had made him reel as if sucker-punched, then prompted him to track her down here, determined to get some answers.

Yet now he hesitated. For all that Angelica was currently trying to appear as if she didn't have a care in the world, she looked tired, he thought, noting the faint shadows beneath her eyes and the strain bracketing her soft, full mouth. Which was hardly a surprise, given the events of the past few months and what he now suspected.

Out of nowhere, he felt a stirring of protectiveness.

Well, great. This was a hell of a time to develop a gallant streak. Nevertheless, he found himself stalling as he tried to think of a way to ease into the subject foremost on his mind. "We need to talk about Mike," he improvised. "I guess you must be upset about everything that's happened—"

"Upset?" A glimmer oddly like hurt lit her eyes, then vanished with a blink of her dark lashes. "It turns out my brother's death wasn't an accident, and you guess I might be upset?" She struggled for control. When she found it, her expression turned coolly indifferent. "Go away, Riley. Please. Just...go away."

His jaw tightened. For as long as he could remember, his motto had been *no regrets, no explanations, no apologies.* Yet for some inexplicable reason, he found he couldn't remain silent. Not with her. "I didn't kill him, Angelica."

She stared at him a moment, then gave a faint sigh and nodded. "For what it's worth, I believe you. So if that's all you wanted..." Although her voice was offhand, a slight tremor shook her fingers as she tucked a wayward strand of hair behind her ear. "I'll be going. It's late, I'm tired and I want to go home."

The vulnerability revealed by that shaking hand rocked him. Almost as much as her matter-of-fact assertion of his innocence. He'd just assumed that everybody in town except for his family thought he was guilty. The discovery that Angelica of all people believed in him was more than he could immediately take in. So much so that it took a second to register when she turned in the direction of her car and started to walk away.

He reached out without thinking and caught her by the arm. "Angel, wait."

A shudder went through her at his touch and she jerked away. "What do you want?" she demanded impatiently.

"I know you're pregnant."

She went utterly still and in that instant, without her ever saying a word, he knew it was true. The confirmation made him feel light-headed. While part of him fiercely welcomed the idea of a child, another part despaired of the timing and the circumstances, and had hoped, for both their sakes, it wasn't true.

But at least Angelica didn't add injury to insult by trying to deny it. On the contrary; she took a deep breath, drew herself up and said with a trace of defiance, "So?"

So? He was going to be a father and all she had to say was *so?* He reminded himself he never lost his temper. "Like I said. We need to talk."

She shook her head. "No."

"What do you mean, *no?*"

"I mean my situation isn't your concern."

"Are you trying to tell me I'm not the father?" Try as he might, he couldn't keep a dangerous note out of his voice. "Because I'm warning you, Angelica, it won't wash. If you're pregnant, the baby's mine—and we both know it."

There was no mistaking the sudden spark in her big green eyes. "Oh, I know perfectly well that you're the father, Riley. What I can't believe is that you really think you can just show up and think you have some say in my life. You don't!"

"The hell I don't," he retorted, doing his best to contain his building agitation. "If there's one thing you can count on, it's that we Fortunes take care of our own."

"Then I guess it's just lucky for me that I'm not a Fortune!"

"Maybe not now, but that's going to change."

"Just what is *that* supposed to mean?"

He shrugged. "Isn't it obvious? We'll have to get married. The sooner the better."

She stared at him in astonishment. "If that's your version of a proposal, the answer is no."

"Dammit, Angelica—"

"We made love, then you took off while I was

sleeping and I haven't heard a word from you in three months. You don't get to show up now pretending concern," she said flatly. She raised her chin. "And now, if you'll excuse me, I'm leaving. Before I say something we'll both really regret." She turned and took a step away, then stopped, looking back at him over her shoulder. "And just so there's no misunderstanding—I don't want to see you again." Not waiting to hear his reply, she walked resolutely toward her car.

Face set, Riley stayed where he was, unable to think of a way to stop her from leaving short of chasing her down and wrestling her to the ground. And while it was tempting, he'd never laid an unwanted hand on a woman in his life—and he wasn't about to start now.

Still, it cost him to stay where he was, to do nothing as she climbed into her car, her ancient Chevy coughed to anemic life and she drove out of the parking lot.

He reached down and picked up the dark green cotton apron she'd dropped in her agitation, balling it in his fist. Not until her taillights had faded from sight did he finally stride toward his Corvette.

No matter what Angelica thought, this wasn't over, he thought grimly.

Not by a long shot.

In the past few weeks he'd lost an alarming portion of his freedom, his faith in the justice system and what had been left of his reputation.

No matter what it took, he wasn't about to lose

his son or daughter, too. And since Angelica was part of the package...

She'd just have to be persuaded to give him another chance.

Spoiled, arrogant, overbearing jerk!

Hands clasped tightly around the steering wheel, Angelica drove toward home on autopilot, her thoughts spinning as erratically as a desert whirlwind.

Damn Riley Fortune! In her entire life, she'd never met anyone with so much nerve. How dare he think he could just show up, crook one of those long, clever fingers and she'd do whatever he wanted? Even if she had done exactly that at their last meeting....

But she was smarter now. Smarter, stronger, not nearly so naive. What did she care that he looked like a fallen angel, with his inky hair, those pale, guarded eyes and that moody, sensual mouth? Or that once upon a time she'd been foolish enough to think that beneath his jaded manner was a man who cared far more about things than he ever let on?

She was done kidding herself. She'd let down her guard once and look where that had gotten her. After nearly twenty-eight years of living like a nun in a vain attempt to live down the Dodd reputation, she was going to be an unwed mother.

And all because she'd made a pair of foolish mistakes, thinking she was in love—and that Riley actually cared for her. She bit her lip against a wave of pained self-disgust, yet she couldn't seem to stop herself from thinking back to the beginning, to the events that had brought them together, however briefly.

It had started innocently enough, on one of those warm, sunny February days for which Arizona was so famous. She'd had a rare night off, and had decided to drop by the Children's Hospital construction site to see if Mike wanted to get a bite to eat after work. She'd meant it as a peace offering, to make up for the way their get-together the previous weekend had ended.

When Mike had initially announced he'd been hired to work on the hospital project for Fortune Construction, Angelica had been more than pleased—she'd been relieved. Her little brother might be clever and able to do anything with his hands, but trouble always seemed to follow him, and in the six years he'd worked construction he'd been fired as often as he'd been hired. Usually it had been for minor things—being tardy, borrowing tools, making smart remarks to the boss. But twice that she'd known of he'd been let go for more serious misdeeds, like padding his hours and taking kickbacks from suppliers.

Yet with the Fortune job, he seemed to have changed. He'd appeared to be making a real effort, and Angelica, who'd struggled single-handedly to raise him after their parents died, had started to think that maybe she hadn't failed him after all; that maybe all he'd needed to succeed was a chance to grow up.

Or so she'd thought, until after dinner the Sunday

night before he'd died, when he'd glanced pointedly around her apartment and said disparagingly, "This place is too damn small."

She'd tried not to be offended. After all, her place *was* tiny. Of course, it was also clean and cozy, and a huge step up from the rundown trailer in which they'd grown up. "It's not *that* bad," she'd said lightly.

Mike, who despite her protests had imbibed several beers more than was wise, had snorted. "It's a dump, Ange. But don't you worry. Another few months, once my ship comes in, I'll get you something really nice. How'd you like to live in one of those big houses out at Saguaro Springs?"

She'd stared at him, all of her big-sister alarms going off. "What are you talking about?"

A sly, cat-who-ate-the-canary smile had flitted across his face. "Let's just say the fat cats are about to get a little lesson in profit sharing."

Her dismay had to have been obvious. "What does that mean? You're not planning on doing anything that might jeopardize your job, are you?"

His smile had vanished. "Dammit, is my damn job all you ever worry about?"

"Of course not. But—"

"Just forget it, okay?" His expression had turned sulky.

"But—"

"I said forget it!" Lurching to his feet, he'd stomped toward the door. "I gotta go."

"Mike, wait—"

He'd glanced back at her over his shoulder.

"You're such a frigging prude, Ange, you know that?" She must've winced at the words, because just for a moment his face had softened. "But thanks for dinner anyway." He'd departed without another word.

In the days that had followed, she'd replayed their conversation a number of times, doing her best to convince herself she'd overreacted and jumped to the wrong conclusion. After all, he wasn't a kid anymore—he had to know that any mistake he made now would be taken seriously, not treated like a mere juvenile matter. Surely he wouldn't do anything foolish.

Yet deep down she hadn't been one-hundred percent sure. So she'd gone out to the job, hoping to take Mike to dinner and diplomatically clarify the matter.

She'd never gotten the chance. Instead, shortly after she'd spotted him on an upper floor and they'd exchanged a wave and a shouted hello, he'd stepped into the temporary service elevator, which seconds later had come crashing down. Dazed and horrified, she'd stood paralyzed as alarms sounded and dust swirled and men shouted, racing from all over the construction site to see what had happened.

And then miraculously Riley had been there, shielding her from the terrible sight of the crumpled elevator cage, leading her away, cradling her against him as her disbelief gave way to grief and hysteria.

She'd been desperate not to think about what had just happened, so every detail of those next few minutes was burned into her mind. She remembered the steely hardness of his body, a shock since he always looked so elegant in his fashionable clothes. She remembered how warm and satiny his skin had felt as she'd buried her face in the open V of his shirt. She could still feel his hands rubbing slowly up and down her back and the press of his cheek against her hair, as well as the soothing rumble of his voice. She recalled his scent, something dark and heady and masculine that had made her want to press closer, breathe deeper, stand there forever and never open her eyes.

Ridiculous as it seemed now, she'd felt safe. As if she'd finally found the one place on earth where she belonged.

Which just went to prove there was nothing like a tragedy to completely negate a person's normal intelligence. Because if there was one thing she'd known since she was fourteen and had first set eyes on eighteen-year-old Riley Fortune, it was that they had nothing in common. He may have rescued her from a bunch of neighborhood toughs, dazzling her with his good looks as he leapt from his shiny sports car and stalked to her defense like a modern Sir Galahad, but even so she'd known he wasn't for the likes of her. There had been so much distance financially, socially and emotionally between the Dodds and the Fortunes, she and Riley might as well have been from different planets.

Nor had anything changed.

He came from money and everything it provided: a beautiful home, plentiful food, nice clothes, an excellent education.

She'd grown up in a rusting travel trailer parked on a vacant lot on the wrong side of town. By the age of eight she'd been adept at feeding herself and her little brother from donations from the local food bank and dressing them out of various charity bins.

Riley's family was powerful and well respected. His father was an influential business leader and his mother revered for her community service. His sister Isabelle's picture was always showing up in the style sections of the Tucson and Pueblo newspapers, while his twin brother, Shane, was a doctor, for heaven's sake.

In stark contrast, her parents had excelled at avoiding gainful employment, at sleeping around and at getting enough from public assistance to keep them well supplied in alcohol and cigarettes. Although she'd grieved when they'd died in a car accident when she was eighteen, she'd had no illusions. No one with an ounce of sense would ever mistake them for role models.

But even knowing all that, it hadn't stopped her from clinging to Riley like an anchor in a storm the day of Mike's accident. She'd *depended* on him. And he, known in their little corner of Arizona as one of the least dependable Fortunes, had stood by her as the paramedics, the police and the medical examiner came and went. He'd insisted on seeing her home and refused to leave her alone until one of her girlfriends arrived.

Nor had his chivalry ended there. Over the next few days he'd helped her with everything from insurance claims to funeral arrangements, brushing off her thanks and claiming he was simply doing his job as Fortune Construction's vice president of Finance.

Which didn't explain why he'd volunteered to keep her company in the limo on the day of the funeral. Or why he'd stood beside her at the cemetery and stayed close during the memorial gathering he'd arranged at the Saguaro Springs Country Club afterward. Much less why he'd seemed genuinely concerned when it all started to catch up with her.

"Come on," he'd said quietly, laying a warm, long-fingered hand to the small of her back as they'd stood on the clubhouse terrace, watching the sun begin its descent. "You look exhausted. Let me take you home."

And she had. She'd let him drive her home, she'd invited him in and she'd let him take her to bed. And as much as she'd like to pretend that he'd taken advantage of her, exploiting her at a vulnerable time, she knew she shared equally in whatever blame was to be assigned.

She'd let herself forget that he was a Fortune and she was a Dodd. She'd been foolish enough to believe she was falling love. And she'd wanted him. As much—if not more—than he'd wanted her.

And now there were consequences to pay.

Choking back a little cry that was half sob and half self-deprecating chuckle, she pulled into the weedy gravel strip that comprised the parking lot for her small walk-up apartment. Bringing the car to a stop, she switched off the lights and engine, and forced herself to repeat the words that had become her mantra every since she'd found out she was pregnant.

I can handle this. I'm young, strong and healthy. So what if I don't have lots of money? I can support myself and my child. I don't have to take charity. Not anymore.

Plus, she had a plan, she reminded herself as she got out of the car and walked tiredly up the rickety stairs to her door. In three weeks time, not only should she have the last of Mike's affairs settled, but she would have completed her semester finals at the University of Arizona at Tucson, where she was a senior. Once she had her diploma, she would be free to go somewhere where no one knew her and carve out a new life for herself and her child.

As for Riley...she was sure he'd get over it. Heck, once he had time to think about it and recover from the shock of not getting his way, he'd probably be relieved.

Right. That's why he asked you to marry him. Because he doesn't care about anyone but himself.

Suddenly angry, she told herself fiercely not to defend him. He didn't need it—he could clearly take care of himself.

Despite the way her hands were shaking, she managed to get her door unlocked. She walked inside. There was a scrabble of toenails on the linoleum, and then she felt a moist, familiar pressure as Cosmo nudged her arm and pressed his nose against her palm.

For all that she welcomed the big dog's enthusiastic greeting, tonight it seemed to emphasize how alone she was. Out of nowhere, she felt a searing ache as she finally let herself consider what it would be like to be Riley's wife, if only he wanted her for herself.

The anger that had sustained her vanished. Leaning back against the door for support, she clamped her teeth down on her lower lip, overcome by an overwhelming sense of desolation.

Yet as much as she hurt, she stubbornly refused to cry. The tears she'd shed over Riley Fortune three months ago had been enough to last a lifetime.

Two

"So. How are you? Really?"

Riley nudged the refrigerator door shut with his hip and cautioned himself to be patient. After all, it wasn't as if the question came as a surprise. He'd been expecting it in one form or another ever since Shane had shown up. While his brother had claimed he'd just happened to be driving by and had decided to drop in, Riley had known instantly this was no impromptu visit.

And he was ready with an answer. "I'm okay." He set a pair of long-necked beers on his gleaming black granite kitchen counter.

"Yeah?"

"Yeah. It helps that I've got the best attorney in Arizona working on my case."

A gleam ignited in Shane's dark eyes at the reference to his new bride, Cynthia, only to fade as he continued to scrutinize his brother. "Right. But if you're so okay, how come you look like hell?"

"Thanks a lot."

"Sorry, Ry, but it's the truth. If I had to make a diagnosis, I'd say you hadn't had a decent night's sleep for a while."

"So?" Riley popped the caps on the beers, came around the end of the counter and handed one to his brother, who was ensconced on the long, glove-soft cream-colored leather sofa in Riley's family room. "I shouldn't have to tell you this, bro—" he took a sip from his own bottle as he settled into a low, oversize taupe-and-burgundy brocade chair "—but there are some damn good reasons for losing sleep that don't have a thing to do with my legal situation."

Shane wasn't buying it. "Yeah? Is that why you've sent enough flowers to Angelica Dodd in the past week to build a float for the Rose Parade?"

Riley frowned. "How'd you hear about that?"

"I'm a doctor, remember? I have patients, and patients like to talk."

"Yeah, well, they shouldn't. And you shouldn't listen."

"What can I say?" Shane's calm expression didn't change. "You're my brother. I care about you. Of course I'm going to listen."

Riley winced, his irritation replaced by a familiar sense of chagrin. Shane was just so caring, so decent, so patient, so good.

He, on the other hand…wasn't.

Just like that, three-plus decades of transgressions flashed through his mind.

According to their mother, Shane had slept through the night at three days old, while Riley had fussed from midnight to dawn for his first nine months.

As toddlers, Shane had played contentedly with whatever was put in front of him, while Riley had chased disaster, scaling kitchen cabinets, sipping shampoo, dismantling playpens and safety gates, falling out windows.

Shane's early report cards had been filled with A's and raves about how he worked well with others. Riley's had contained C's and D's and tart comments about his failure to apply himself.

By the time they'd reached their teens, Shane, an honor student, had already known he wanted to be a doctor and had been deeply interested in learning about their Native American heritage. Riley, who'd been belatedly diagnosed with a reading disability, had struggled with every subject except math. Worse—at least from his family's standpoint—he hadn't cared. The only thing that had interested *him* had been the opposite sex.

Looking back, he supposed it was a miracle that despite their differences, he and Shane were such good friends. But then, while they didn't look alike except for their inky hair—their Papaguo heritage was stamped on his brother's face while Riley's features came from their Anglo mother's side of the family—they were bound together by thirty-two years of shared history.

"So." Shane's quiet voice interrupted his thoughts. "Are you going to answer my question or not?"

Riley regarded him blankly. "What question?"

Shane sighed. "Do you or don't you have something going with Angelica Dodd?"

Riley hesitated, but just for a second. "Look, I'd rather the rest of the family didn't know this yet, but yeah. We're getting married."

"What!" Shane's jaw dropped, and then he caught himself and his expression turned apologetic. "Sorry. I didn't mean—that is, that's great."

"Forget the diplomacy. She's pregnant."

"How the hell did that happen?"

Riley shook his head in mock disgust. "And you call yourself a doctor. Guess."

"That's not what I meant and you know it. It's just that you're always so damn careful. All these years, you've been adamant about not taking any chances. You're the last person I'd expect this to happen to."

Riley shrugged, not about to admit that he'd surprised himself, too. Much less confess that the host of emotions he'd felt that night—tenderness, protectiveness, possessiveness—had been as out of character as his actions.

But then, from the day of Mike's accident, nothing had gone the way he'd expected. All of their lives, Shane had been the steady, dependable one. So it was no great surprise that Riley had been caught completely off guard when Angelica had turned to him to protect and support her. But she had, clinging to him as if he were her only port in an angry sea.

And he'd liked it.

And then afterward…well, hell. She'd just been so damn alone. It hadn't been any sweat off his back to take care of a few little things for her. And she'd been so damn grateful. She hadn't said very much, but the way she'd looked at him had made him feel as if he were some sort of knight in shining armor.

They both should have known better.

Not that it was any big deal, he was quick to assure himself. But still… "Hey, what can I say?" He forced a smile. "I'm human. I screwed up. Now all I can do is try to make things right."

If Shane recognized the irony in *that,* he didn't let on. "Yeah, but marriage… It's a huge step. Are you sure?"

"Yeah. I know it's hard to believe—" he couldn't keep a touch of sarcasm out of his voice "—but even I have some standards. I want my kid to have my name. And I want to be sure—if justice doesn't prevail—that he or she doesn't suffer."

"Hey, come on," Shane protested. "It's a bogus charge, and we both know it. And sooner or later, so will everyone else."

"Maybe. Maybe not," Riley retorted. "But I can't afford to wait and see, can I?"

Shane reluctantly shook his head. "No. I suppose not. So when's the big date?"

"I don't know. There are still some...details...we have to iron out."

"Like what?"

He made a vague gesture. "You know—the usual. Figuring out where and when. Getting Angelica to say yes."

Shane choked on his beer. "Excuse me?"

"It's no big deal," Riley said quickly. Too quickly. He forced himself to relax. "She just needs some time to think about it. Once she does, she'll come around," he added with more confidence than he felt.

Because what Shane didn't know—and Riley wasn't about to tell him—was that Angelica had taken all the pricey bouquets he'd sent her and had donated them to the senior citizens center. And she'd refused delivery of the diamond earrings and bracelet he'd sent her, as well as the delicate gold necklace with the emerald pendant meant to flatter her eyes—much to the jeweler's ire. What's more, not only wouldn't she take his phone calls, she'd flatly refused to wait on him the past three nights when he'd sat in her section at the Camel Corral.

Unaccustomed to rejection, he felt a surge of frustration just thinking about it. "She will," he repeated stubbornly.

Shane cleared his throat, and with an inner curse, Riley saw the knowing look in his twin's eyes and realized he must not be doing as good a job hiding his feelings as he thought. Yet to his relief, all Shane said was, "You want a piece of advice?"

Chagrined to realize he actually did, he shrugged. "Sure. Why not?"

"Forget the flowers. Go talk to her. Face-to-face. Tell her how you feel." He glanced at his watch, set his half-full beer down on the coffee table and climbed to his feet. "And now, I've got to run. I promised Cynthia I'd fix dinner tonight."

"Be sure to give her my sympathy."

Shane grinned over his shoulder as he started for the front of the house. "You should talk. Give my regards to your TV dinner."

A moment later Riley heard the front door open and shut.

Shaking his head, he took another sip of his beer and gazed out through the sliding glass door at the bright blend of pink, scarlet and white flowers in the huge terracotta pots clustered around his sweeping terrace. Off in the distance, a hawk soared against the brilliant blue bowl of the sky, gliding and swooping as it rode the thermal drafts rising off the desert.

Riley sighed. He'd been waiting, hoping Angelica would give him some sign she was coming around, but as usual, Shane was right. It was time to quit sitting on his hands and take action.

And this time would be different from the last.

Because this time, no matter what it took, he meant to convince her to be his wife.

The knock on the door brought Angelica's head up.

Seated cross-legged on the worn rug in her living

room, she pushed a strand of hair off her hot, flushed cheek and surveyed the untidy stacks of Mike's things spread out before her. So far there was a pocketknife, a packet of photographs, a handful of wrenches and screwdrivers, a sheaf of old bills and what had to be five years of bank statements.

One down, ten to go, she thought with a tired glance at the cardboard boxes still stacked in the corner of the apartment's minuscule dining area. In the weeks after Mike's death, she'd had no choice but to dispose of his more substantial belongings—his clothes and stereo, his car, the guitar she'd bought him for his seventeenth birthday. Everything else she'd boxed up and set aside with every intention of going through it later.

But she hadn't. And though she wanted to believe the reason she'd put it off stemmed from a fear that once it was done she'd lose her last link with her brother, deep down she suspected she also feared what she might find.

Because try as she might, she couldn't forget her final conversation with Mike, and the alarm she'd felt when he'd claimed his ship was about to come in. In the months since, she must've gone over that conversation a hundred times, trying to convince herself that he'd just been spouting off, making a meaningless boast brought on by too much alcohol.

But still, she wondered. Had he been involved in something shady? Could it have something to do with his death? And—knowing her little brother's tendency to always hedge his bets—was it possible he'd left behind some kind of evidence detailing what he was involved in? Something the police might have missed, since they'd initially believed his death to be an accident?

Angelica sighed. Whatever the truth, she supposed she was going to find out, since her decision to leave town meant she couldn't put off going through his things any longer.

There was another sharp rap on the door.

"Hold on! I'm coming!" She climbed to her feet, praying it was the super, here to finally fix the air conditioner. The unit had been on the fritz for two days, the same length of time as the current unseasonable heat wave. Today's high had to be near ninety, and her small portable fan wasn't doing a thing to alleviate the heat that had collected in her apartment.

Dusting her hands on her ragged cutoffs, she tugged down her faded blue T-shirt and yanked the door open. "Thank goodness—" She froze, staring in dismay at the man standing there.

Riley.

"Hi." Despite the heat, he looked as cool as an icy drink, dressed as he was in a sleek ivory V-neck T-shirt, khaki slacks and a pair of brown leather sandals that probably cost more than her monthly rent.

"What do you want?" To her disgust, his silver spoon elegance made her feel about as appealing as an unwashed sweat sock.

"Can I come in?"

"*No.*"

He ignored her and strolled forward, leaving her

no choice but to give way or have him press up against her.

With a huff of annoyance, she moved aside, staunchly ignoring the way her stomach tightened as she caught a hint of his cologne—elusive, expensive, tantalizingly familiar—as he passed by. She crossed her arms and turned to face him, pointedly leaving the door open. "I'd like you to leave. Now."

Clearly disturbed by her tone, Cosmo, who was sleeping in a patch of sunlight by the window across the room, raised his big, shaggy head. Everybody's buddy, the dog briefly regarded Riley, apparently decided the man was no threat, flopped down and went back to sleep.

"We need to talk," Riley said.

"I don't think so."

"I do." His gaze skimmed over the room, lingered a moment on the small eating bar that separated the kitchen from the living room, then slowly came back to rest on her face.

And just like that, she found herself remembering the last time they'd been here together. And how, after he'd stripped her down to her bra and panties, Riley had lifted her up onto that same eating bar, wedged himself between her thighs, tipped her head back with a tug to her hair and found her exposed throat with his hot, clever mouth.

She'd been so aroused she'd felt faint.

"Look." Gritting her teeth at the husky note in her voice, she stopped and cleared her throat. "I thought I made myself clear the other night. I don't want to see you.''

"That was a mistake.''

"What was a mistake?''

"It was late, and you must've been exhausted after spending all those hours on your feet. I shouldn't have ambushed you that way.''

Riley Fortune was apologizing? She stared at him warily.

"I should've waited, chosen a better time and place for us to talk. I upset you, and I'm sorry, but I've been trying all week to make up for it.''

"By doing what? Harassing me at work? Trying to buy me?'' The words were out before she could stop herself.

He sent her a wounded look. "Of course not. I just wanted you to understand that I'm not giving up.''

Incredibly, Angelica felt a pang of guilt. Part of her was still beyond angry at his apparent belief that he could breeze in and out of her life at his whim. But there was another, no-doubt foolish part, that was just the teensiest bit flattered he'd gone to the trouble to seek her out, to send her all those flowers and that beautiful jewelry.

Not because she thought she deserved it. But because Riley simply didn't pursue women.

He didn't have to.

Gosh—and that means what? That you're willing to overlook his previous vanishing act? Or forget that no matter how gorgeous the package, he's six feet, two inches of trouble?

Not likely. "You might want to reconsider," she said coolly, raising her voice slightly as a door banged in the adjoining apartment, followed by the sound of voices and a television coming on. "Because no matter what you do, I'm not about to be pressured—"

"Aw, come on." To her amazement, he had the nerve to sound amused. "Give me a little credit. If I were trying to pressure you, it wouldn't be with flowers. I could've raised hell when you refused to serve me at the Corral, and it's a good bet they would've fired you. Or I could've called Burt Henner, who owns this place and offered him a deal on a renovation. God knows, the place needs it. And don't think it hasn't occurred to me that you might be more inclined to listen to reason if you didn't have a job or place to live."

She raised her chin, glad all over again that she planned to leave town. "Don't bet on it."

"All right." With a little shock she saw that in stark contrast to his jocular manner, there wasn't a speck of amusement in his silver eyes. "So why don't we cut to the chase? What *is* it going to take to win you over? Am I going to have to get down on my knees and beg?"

It was a very tempting image. Or would've been, if not for the memory it instantly conjured of him kneeling before her in her bedroom, his hands cradling her waist, his tongue circling her navel...

The heat was suddenly stifling. Belatedly aware of the early evening sunshine beating down on her from the open doorway, she flicked the door shut, only to instantly regret the impulsive action as she turned back to Riley and the room seemed to shrink. "Why are you doing this?" she demanded. "Is it guilt about Mike? Or are you afraid that somebody like me couldn't bring up a Fortune properly?"

"Dammit, Angelica, of course not! I'm trying to do the right thing. For me, for you, for our baby."

"That doesn't mean we have to get married!"

"Yes, it does."

"Why?"

"Because." He raked a hand through his hair as he considered his answer. "Did you know my parents weren't married until Shane and I were three? They'd been high school sweethearts, but when my mom found out after graduation that she was pregnant, she didn't tell my dad, not wanting to wreck his college plans. She thought she was doing the right thing, but it doesn't change the fact that my father missed the first three years of our lives."

"I don't see what that has to do with our situation."

"Just listen. Last month, my brother discovered history had repeated itself, that *he* had a son. Lucky for him, he also discovered that he and the boy's mother still love each other, but he'll never get those lost years back. I don't have any intention of making the same mistake. Not if I don't have to."

"It's not that simple," she said stubbornly. "The way I grew up—" She swallowed as she felt the familiar shame. "My parents had a miserable marriage." She could see by his expression that she wasn't telling him anything he didn't already know.

But then, Jack and Evelyn Dodd had spent most of their time hanging out in local bars, so their numerous infidelities, as well as their alcohol-fueled fights, were public knowledge. "It wasn't a very happy situation, for anyone. I want something better than that for my child."

"And you think being raised by a single mother, branded as illegitimate, cut off from grandparents, aunts, uncles and cousins, is it?" he demanded incredulously.

"No! Of course not. But—"

"And what about me? Am I just supposed to fade away? Pretend I don't have a son or daughter? Because I'm telling you, sweetheart, it's not going to happen."

Angelica blinked, stunned by the absolute resolve in his voice. Until the past few moments, she'd assumed he was just going through the motions, offering to marry her because it was the sort of thing a Fortune was expected to do.

But not now. Hearing the determination in his voice—and seeing it in his handsome, compelling face—she knew she'd miscalculated in the worst possible way. She should've realized that Riley always did precisely what he wanted. That he wouldn't have reappeared in her life for anything less than his own personal convictions.

And that he wasn't likely to go away just because she wanted him to.

She bit her lip, struck by the irony of the situation. Three months ago she'd have given anything for his attention. Now she had it, but for all the wrong reasons.

"Marry me," he said forcefully. "You'll have a beautiful house, no money worries, plenty of time to do nothing but care for yourself and the baby. You won't have to work unless you want to. I won't insult your intelligence by promising to be the perfect husband, but I swear I'll do my best to never publicly embarrass you."

To her shock, she realized she believed him. And that for the first time she was actually considering his proposal. "What about your family?"

"They'll be thrilled I'm finally settling down."

Angelica seriously doubted that. It was much more likely that once they learned she was pregnant they'd think she'd trapped him into marriage. Which was nothing compared to what they'd think if it turned out Mike had been involved in something he shouldn't have been.

And yet... In all the ways that mattered, she'd been alone for so long. It would be a relief to have the kind of security Riley was offering, to actually *belong* somewhere for a change. And there was always a chance, however slim, that given some time they might become a real family. Most important of all, he was right about the advantages for their baby. Enough that the case could be made that she had an obligation to at least *try* to make a union between them work.

"All right." Amazingly, she sounded calm despite the painful way her heart was thumping. "I'll marry you."

It seemed to take a moment for her words to register. "You will?"

"Yes." She waited, expecting to see a look of triumph.

It didn't come. Instead, his enigmatic gaze searched her face, something she couldn't define transforming his eyes from silver to smoke. He cleared his throat. "I'll be a good father, Angelica—I swear. As for us—" A brief, sardonic smile lit his face as he gave a slight, dismissive shrug. "Maybe you'll get lucky, the D.A. will get his way and I won't be around."

Her breath caught at the hint of vulnerability she could have sworn she'd heard in his voice.

But all she said was, "Maybe I will."

Three

Once upon a time, as a romantic teenager who'd wanted to believe in happily ever afters, Angelica had daydreamed about her wedding day.

She'd envisioned a hushed church, awash in candlelight and the sweet scent of camellias. She'd pictured herself in an exquisite white dress encrusted with seed pearls and lace, the full skirt billowing around her as she held out her hand and her groom—gentle, handsome, adoring—slipped a burnished gold wedding band on her finger. To seal their vows, he'd cup her face in his hand and they'd exchange a tender kiss that spoke of love, respect and mutual understanding.

Another adolescent fantasy shot to pieces, she thought as Judge Melvin's deep, sonorous voice flowed over her. Oh, some of the words were familiar—she and Riley had promised to "love, honor, cherish and protect each other, forsaking all others." They'd also exchanged rings, the look of surprise on Riley's face as she'd produced a wedding band for him to wear well worth the hit to her savings account. And he did look handsome, his black hair and sun-kissed skin set off by natural-colored linen pants, a natural-colored silk shirt open at the throat and an exquisitely fitted taupe sport coat.

But that was where all resemblance to what she'd once imagined ended.

The judge was currently going on about how two very different threads woven in opposite directions could form a beautiful tapestry or something to that effect.

Instead of a church, the ceremony was taking place at His Honor's house. While the interior courtyard room where they were gathered was lovely, with its cool tile floor, bubbling fountain and profusion of potted flowers, no one would ever mistake it for a place of worship.

Just as no one was likely to confuse her pale yellow suit, borrowed from a girlfriend for her upcoming college graduation, and far from a perfect fit, for a real wedding dress.

Not that she had anyone to blame but herself. It had been her decision to have a small civil ceremony, no fuss, no muss. And no one but the judge's modest staff of secretary and housekeeper to act as witnesses, since she didn't feel anywhere near to ready to face the Fortune family. Particularly when she didn't have anyone of her own to attend.

"Are you sure?" Riley had asked when she'd stated her preferences. The two of them had been standing in her living room, the conversation having turned to practical considerations once she'd finally agreed to marry him.

"Yes. Under the circumstances, I'd prefer to keep things simple. Unless, of course, you're afraid it will upset your family."

"No. This is between us. Whatever you want is fine." He'd reached out as if to give her shoulder a squeeze and she'd instinctively stepped back, stopping him in his tracks. A flicker of surprise had danced across his face. "What's the matter?"

"Nothing. I just—" *don't want you to touch me.*

The realization had frozen her in place. Yet it had only taken her an instant to decide her reaction made perfect sense. The last time he'd put his hands on her she'd completely lost her head. And though she wanted to believe her lapse of judgement had been due to her being off-balance because of Mike's death, she wasn't one-hundred per cent sure.

Not when just being in the same room with Riley made her more than a little breathless.

"Angelica?" His questioning voice had drawn her back.

"I just...everything's happening so fast," she'd hedged. "I guess I need some time to get used to the idea."

Silence. And then he'd given one of those negligent little shrugs she was starting to consider his trademark. "Sure. No problem."

She glanced down now at the gold and diamond wedding set glittering on the third finger of her left hand. And told herself—the way she had repeatedly the past three days, as she'd hastily packed up her apartment, trying to shake of a sense of unreality when Riley insisted on sending someone to transport her things since he didn't want her lifting anything heavy—that she could handle this.

Obviously, she found Riley physically attractive. Just as clearly, she wanted this marriage to work, since it went against her hard-won principles to enter such a union planning for the day when it would prove a bust and she'd take her child and walk away.

But... She had no intention of letting such hopes get in the way of her common sense. Any more than she intended to sacrifice what was left of her self-respect.

As Riley had made crystal clear, first when he'd bolted after they made love and then again when he'd proposed, this wasn't a love match. And that made it essential that she behave with dignity and restraint, making it clear she expected to be treated as an equal partner.

Even if it wasn't going to be easy. Not, she thought, sneaking a peek at him, when something as innocent as the sight of his profile—lean, chiseled, the cheek creased with a faint groove that she knew hid a devastating dimple—made her pulse pick up.

"...and by the power vested in me by the state of Arizona, I now pronounce you husband and wife.'' The judge's announcement grabbed her attention. She shifted her gaze to him, just in time to see him smile indulgently at Riley. "Young man, you may kiss the bride.''

Her lips parted in instinctive protest. And then she caught herself. Given that they were married now, she might as well get this over with. The sooner she proved she could handle herself, the better she'd feel.

Forcing a smile, she turned toward her new husband, standing her ground as he took a step closer, put his arms around her waist and settled his palms against the small of her back. She took a fortifying breath and raised her chin, determined to meet him halfway as his mouth claimed her own.

A major miscalculation.

She had just enough time for that single thought as delight shuddered through her. And then her mind went blank, instantly and completely overwhelmed by pleasure, while her body responded as if she and Riley had never been apart.

Never had a kiss felt so right. Except for the last time…

A shiver of pure need raced down her spine as the delicious scent that was exclusively his teased her senses. As if of its own volition, one of her hands crept from his shoulder to the bare skin of his neck to greedily explore the satiny patch of skin behind his ear, while the other tangled itself in the cool silk of his hair. The slight pressure of his chest against her breasts was too much and not enough all at once.

His mouth was so hot, so right. She tried to remember, as he traced a circle on her spine with one lazy finger, why she shouldn't slide her hands inside his coat. She knew what she'd find. For all that he looked so sleek and elegant in his pricey clothes, beneath them he was lean, muscular and bronzed. The ultimate hardbody. In more ways than one...

Without warning, Riley lifted his head.

Instantly bereft, a protest trembling on her throbbing lips, Angelica snapped her eyes open—and found herself looking straight into his.

The expression in those silvery depths was dark and intent. "You okay?"

She wasn't, of course. Because even as she forced herself to take a much needed breath and murmur "Yes," dismay threatened to overwhelm her.

She felt naked, no great surprise since their kiss had stripped all pretense away and she knew she'd been kidding herself. Riley's allure was as powerful as ever, while her ability to resist him was... nonexistent. Even now, with her brain at least partially functioning, there was a part of her that wanted nothing more than to drag him off somewhere private and make love.

Yet she also knew there was no way she could give her body without also committing her heart.

And that she wouldn't do.

"*This* is your house?" Angelica said as Riley turned into his circular driveway.

"Yeah." He stopped the car before the portico and turned off the engine.

"But...it's huge."

With a slight shock, he realized she'd never been here before. There'd been no question of it three months ago, of course. And then the past few days, Angelica had seemed so preoccupied with the move—and so insistent on keeping a certain distance between them—it just hadn't come up.

Now, he tried to consider the place he called home through her eyes. A sprawling single-story contemporary on an acre lot, with a three-car garage, a soaring roof line and lots of windows, he supposed it did appear pretty substantial. Particularly when compared to her tiny apartment. "Yeah. I guess it is."

"You live here all by yourself?"

He couldn't keep a trace of irony out of his voice. "Not anymore."

She turned to stare at him and he realized he'd hit a nerve, even if she did sound oh-so-reasonable when she spoke. "Look. If you're having second thoughts about this, just say so. There's no law that says we have to live together. Not yet, anyway. We could always wait until the baby's born. So if you want to make other arrangements—"

"You're kidding, right?" He told himself firmly she had to be. "Wouldn't that sort of defeat the whole purpose of getting married? And didn't we agree this was the right thing to do for our kid?"

Was it his imagination, or did her shoulders sag a little? "Yes. Yes, we did." She looked away. "I don't know what got into me."

That made two of them. He reminded himself of

the need to be patient, never one of his stronger attributes. "Do you want to go in or not?"

"Yes. Of course." With an unconvincing smile, she unlatched her seat belt and reached for the door handle.

Frowning, he followed suit, wondering as he shut his door what her problem was. After all, it wasn't as if he didn't have a few reservations about this marriage himself. He'd just been so focused on convincing her to go through with it, he hadn't devoted any time to thinking about what happened afterward. What happened *now*.

It didn't take a genius to figure out both of them were going to have to make some adjustments, however. Hell, he'd lived alone ever since his twenty-first birthday and he was accustomed to his freedom, to coming and going as he pleased. What's more, he knew he had a tendency to be moody, and that he required a certain amount of time to himself. Nor did he doubt that Angelica had her own quirks and idiosyncrasies.

So he didn't expect this to be easy. But then again, things could be worse. Based on that burn-up-the-rafters kiss they'd shared after the wedding ceremony, it was clear the attraction between them was as hot as ever. Shotgun marriage or not, he was definitely looking forward to their wedding night.

And not just for the pleasure of the experience, either. But because for some reason the one other time they'd spent together had taken on an unwarranted significance in his mind and he was eager to dispel it. Intellectually, he knew without a doubt that the only connection they'd shared had been physical. So why, whenever he let himself think about that night, was an overwhelming sense of belonging the first thing that came to mind?

He shoved his hands in his pockets and hitched his shoulders impatiently, damned if he knew the answer. But he was more than ready to prove that his memory was playing tricks on him. If he also enjoyed himself in the process, well then, so much the better.

He retrieved Angelica's overnight bag from the trunk and headed toward the house, where she stood by one of the oversize ornamental planters that flanked the front door.

She touched a finger to a lush pink blossom. "I didn't know you had a green thumb."

He unlocked the door and pushed it open. "I don't. I have a service that takes care of the yard and pool for me." Like most southern Arizona homes, his didn't have a lawn, which couldn't survive the torrid summers. Instead, artfully placed amidst sections of ornamental rock were a variety of palms, shrubs and potted flowers, all of which required regular care to flourish.

"Oh."

He took a step back, taking advantage of the moment to rest his hand on the small of her back. "After you."

A faint tremor went through her and she promptly stepped into the house—and away from him.

He followed, puzzled and a little annoyed by her skittishness. He set down her bag. Tossing his keys into a crystal bowl that sat on the console table in the foyer, he glanced over at her, his good humor restored as her clear green eyes widened slightly as she took a look around.

Like the rest of the house, the foyer walls were painted a light taupe and trimmed in white. Thick Oriental runners in cream, rose and pale green covered the white marble tile in the entry and hall. To the right was the dining room, where silver and gray upholstered chairs surrounded an oval glass table top supported by a granite pedestal. Down a step to the left was the living room, where a curving ice-green sofa sat intimately before the marble fireplace in a room intended to be both inviting and restful.

"Wow," Angelica said a little breathlessly. "This is really lovely. Did you have a professional decorator?"

"No. I did it myself." At her look of surprise, he couldn't resist a chiding sound. "What? You think chrome and smoked glass are more my style?"

"More like mirrors on the ceiling," she murmured.

He couldn't resist. "Oh, I had those taken out last week. Except," he added silkily, "for the one in my bedroom. Our bedroom, now."

Her gaze flew to his face. He wanted to smile at her dismayed expression—until she bit her lower lip. Suddenly he found himself wondering what would happen if he gave in to temptation, leaned forward and claimed her full, soft mouth.

As if someone had flipped a switch, awareness

stretched between them, electrifying the air in the
foyer like a burst of summer lightning.

Angelica was the first to look away. "If you don't
mind, I could really use a glass of water."

He swallowed, chagrined to find his own throat
was a little dry. "Yeah. That's not a bad idea. Follow me." He led the way down the hall to the family
room and kitchen.

Shrugging out of his sport coat, he tossed it over
one of the tall swivel stools that flanked the far side
of the cooking island and retrieved a pair of glasses
from the cupboard. He set about filling them with
ice and water, all the while keeping an eye on Angelica as she wandered around the room, touching
the burgundy throw draped over the back of the
couch, checking out the titles in the bookcase that
stretched along one wall.

With a slight grimace, he acknowledged that just
looking at her made him feel hot. Oh, she wasn't a
classic beauty by any means—her mouth was too
full, her nose too pert. But her hair, all thick and
glossy as it fell in a silvery-brown sheet of satin past
her shoulders, was a definite turn-on. So was the
way her soft yellow suit skimmed her slim body, for
all that the garment was rather dated.

He wondered suddenly what she had on under it.
A slip? Or just her bra, panties and a pair of thigh-
high nylons, the way she had the last time they'd
been together?

At the memory, his body tightened painfully.
Maybe they shouldn't wait until tonight to enjoy
their wedding night, he decided as he walked over

to join her. After all, there was no rule that said you had to wait for the sun to go down to enjoy yourself. He handed her one of the glasses of water.

"Thanks." She took a sip, then looked out the sliding glass doors, where beams of sunlight glinted off the crystal-blue water of the pool. "I always knew people lived like this," she said quietly. "I just never expected to be one of them."

There was a note of uncertainty in her voice. It made him feel strangely protective, and he moved a step closer. "You'll get used to it. This is your home now and I want you to feel comfortable. Just give it some time."

"I hope you're right." She took another swallow from her glass. A bead of water clung to the corner of her mouth. She licked it off with a flick of her tongue that he felt squarely in his solar plexus.

"I am." He took the glass from her hand and reached past her to set it on the bookcase with his own. When he straightened, only inches separated them. "Trust me."

"Riley—"

"Hmm?" He lowered his head only to encounter empty space as she stepped sideways out of his reach.

"Don't."

He straightened. "Don't what?"

"Don't come on to me."

He made no effort to hide his surprise. "Why not?"

"Because."

"Now that explains a heck of lot."

She flushed. "I'm sorry. I just—I don't—" She hugged her arms to herself and took a deep breath. "I don't think we should...sleep together."

He struggled to keep the dismay off his face. "You're kidding, right?" She had to be.

"I wouldn't kid about something so serious."

That was beginning to sink in. "Yeah, but we're *married.*"

"I know. Trust me, I know. But like I said before, this is all happening so fast. In a lot of ways, we're still strangers. I need a chance to get to know you better before we're... intimate."

He had just enough presence of mind to keep from pointing out that hadn't stopped her the last time. Instead, telling himself he wasn't completely without some charm—and that this was definitely the time to time to employ it—he gently wrapped a silky strand of her hair around his finger and tipped her face up to his. "I agree we need to get better acquainted. But we already know we're physically compatible. Why not use it to our advantage?"

She tugged her hair free of his hold and backed away, raising her hands as if to ward him off. "No."

It was an effort, but he stayed where he was. "At least think about what you'll be missing." *I sure am.*

Those limpid green eyes met his without flinching. "I have. And I still think we should wait."

She really meant it. A jumble of emotions swirled through him. Need. Disappointment. Frustration.

For half a second he almost said to hell with it and hauled her into his arms. Maybe she'd have a change of heart if he reminded her what she was giving up.

And if she didn't?

He abruptly reached past her, grabbed his glass of water, brought it to his lips and drank.

The way things had been going, he should have expected this. Ever since the night they'd spent together his life had been unraveling. This was just more of the same.

He stood accused of murder. He was going to be a father. And now he'd somehow managed to marry the one woman in Pueblo County between eighteen and thirty who didn't want to sleep with him.

And the icing on the cake? She was the only one he wanted. Not that he expected it to always be that way. But, for the moment...

There had to be a way. He just needed some time to decide what it was.

He polished off the water, lowered the glass and dredged up a careless smile. "If that's what you want... All right."

"Really?" She let out her breath. "You understand?"

He didn't understand jack at this point, but he would. "Sure."

"Oh, that's good."

"Good" was hardly the word he'd use to describe it. But somehow he refrained from saying so. Instead, he headed for the kitchen to get another glass of ice water.

It was just too damn bad his pride kept him from pouring it where he needed it most.

Four

The dream started the way it always did.

Angelica was walking slowly up the stairs to her apartment. On some level she knew it wasn't really happening, that she was only reliving the past. And yet, it seemed so immediate, so real...

Cars whizzed past on the street below her. The sun was quickly sinking in the west, and a gentle breeze was blowing in off the desert, chasing away the day's heat.

She barely noticed. Instead, her thoughts were turned inward. Mike, the little brother she'd done her best to raise, was really gone. And though she felt physically drained and inexpressibly sad, she was also relieved that the funeral and the rest of the past week's distressing events were finally over.

She was also deeply grateful to the man one step behind her. She didn't know how she would have survived the past few days without Riley Fortune. Despite his bad-boy reputation, he'd been her hero.

They reached the small landing that fronted her door. Turning, she searched for the words to tell him how much his help had meant to her, then finally gave up. "I'm sorry," she said with an apologetic smile. "But I don't know how to thank you—"

"Forget it," he said immediately, looking uncomfortable.

His reaction didn't surprise her. If there was one thing she'd learned about him the past week, it was that he didn't respond well to gratitude. And yet... "I can't."

There was a protracted silence as they considered each other. He ran a hand through his hair, and her stomach gave an unexpected flutter as the shiny strands slid through his long, graceful fingers. "I should go."

"No," she said instantly, then managed an awkward little laugh at the alarm obvious in her voice. "I'm sorry. I'm just not ready to be alone. Won't you come in? Please? Just for a little while?"

Something flickered in his eyes. "I'm not sure that's a good idea."

"Please?" she repeated.

For a moment she was sure he was going to refuse. Then he shrugged. "All right. For a few minutes."

She unlocked the door. Once inside, she shrugged

out of her inexpensive black suit jacket. "Would you like something to drink? Iced tea? A beer?"

"No, thanks."

"Okay." Rubbing her hands over her arms, she walked across her tiny living room. Now that he was actually here, she couldn't think of a thing to say so she took refuge in action, straightening the fuzzy afghan draped over her old rocking chair, rearranging the small collection of porcelain angels on her inexpensive curio shelf.

She looked over to find him watching her, and there was something in his gaze that made her breath hitch. Suddenly self-conscious, she found herself rushing into speech. "I meant what I said outside. I don't know how to thank you. Or what I would have done this week without you. Everything you did… It made all the difference." As if compelled by something outside of herself, she walked toward him.

He flashed a careless, self-denigrating smile. "I didn't do anything special. At least, not anything that any half-ass decent friend wouldn't do. It's just a surprise coming from me."

She couldn't stand to hear him put himself down. "Don't, Riley, please. Because I really don't think I could have made it w-without you." Her voice cracked, and just like that, the past few days caught up with her. Tears flooded her eyes, and she suddenly couldn't breath for the lump in her throat. Mortified, she started to turn away. "Oh, Lord, I'm sorry…"

There was a pause the length of a heartbeat, and

then she felt his hand close around her upper arm and he was tugging her toward him. "Dammit, Angel. Don't cry. Please."

It seemed like the most natural thing in the world to let him gather her close, to shut her eyes and lean against him. Enveloped by an overwhelming sense of safety, for a moment out of time she didn't think about anything except the comfort of his presence, the solid strength of his arms, the warm press of his cheek against her hair.

But then, at some point, awareness prickled to life.

She grew more and more conscious of the heat of his lean body beneath his stylish Armani suit, as well as his strong, steady heartbeat. She felt his breath tickling her cheek, his thighs pressing against hers, the weight of his hands resting against the base of her spine.

She raised her head, looked into his eyes and suddenly felt dizzy with wanting him. She let out a strangled breath. "Oh. My. Riley."

He stared back and she knew, even before he spoke, that he wanted her, too. "Yeah. I know."

The unexpected note of uncertainty in his voice gave her courage. "Make love to me."

"Are you sure?"

"Yes." Still, he hesitated, and with a boldness totally unlike herself, she took his hand and pressed it to her throat. "Touch me," she whispered.

His eyes never leaving hers, he stroked his thumb over the hollow at her collarbone. Then slowly, with fingers bedeviled by the faintest tremor, he unbuttoned her blouse and peeled it off. Next her skirt fluttered to the floor, leaving her standing before him in her bra and panties, her high heels and the thigh-high nylons that were her answer to the warm Arizona weather.

She lifted her chin, proud of her body for the first time ever as his gaze poured over her like liquid silver. The only other time she'd been with a man, it had been a major disappointment.

There was nothing disappointing about Riley.

"You sure about this?" he asked intently.

"Yes." She watched breathlessly as he shed his clothes with all the grace of a Hollywood matinee idol, revealing a body that was strong and lean, with clearly delineated biceps and triceps and a washboard stomach. Between his long, powerful thighs, his sex rose straight and thick, unabashedly masculine.

She'd never felt like this in her life. She wanted to touch him. She wanted to rub her cheek over the bronzed skin of his abdomen, run her fingertips over the fine cross-hatching of hair on his legs and arms, press her aching breasts against his smooth, muscular chest, measure the velvety hardness of him between her palms.

She wanted him to touch her, too. She wanted to feel his hands everywhere against her bare skin, experience the tug of his mouth at her breast, know what it felt like to have his body molded to hers.

In the next instant longing became reality as he stepped toward her, grasped her around the waist and lifted her effortlessly onto the pass-through into the kitchen. Gripping his arms for balance, she groaned as his mouth latched onto hers.

It was too much and not enough. Instinctively wrapping her legs around his waist, she couldn't stop the sob that tore through her as he slicked his thumb over the slippery center of her desire. "Oh. Oh!"

He groaned. "Angel, you're so damn sweet—"

"Love me, Riley," she said insistently.

She shuddered at his first powerful thrust. Pleasure slammed through her, unexpected, overpowering, unlike anything she'd ever known.

She called his name and his arms tightened around her, his body rocked, and then he, too, was crying out. "Angel. Baby. Ah. Ah, damn—!"

Angelica bolted awake, her heart pounding, her body throbbing. For a second she wasn't quite sure where she was. All she knew was that she ached with a bewildering combination of satisfaction...and need.

For Riley. For his touch and his kisses. For the sound of his voice saying her name and the hard slide of his body against hers, inside hers...

She let out a breathless sob. Yet as the seconds passed, her mind began to clear and she knew it had all been just a dream. She wasn't in her bedroom at her apartment following Mike's funeral, but at Riley's house in a spare room, on what was technically her wedding night.

The thought had her scrambling free of the covers as if the mattress were on fire. Desperately seeking escape, she hurried across the room, yanked open the sliding glass door and fled outside, seeking comfort in the vastness of the night.

She didn't stop her flight until she reached the railing at the far side of the patio. Jerking to a halt, she pushed the hair off her damp face and took a deep breath, grateful for the cool air as it skimmed across her overheated skin.

She looked up at the dense spangling of stars overhead, willing the past to recede. Yet it was as if she'd opened a window that wouldn't shut; try as she might, she couldn't refrain from thinking about the rest of the night she and Riley had spent together.

After that first hungry coupling, he'd picked her up and carried her into her bedroom. She wasn't sure what she'd expected, but it hadn't been the tender way he'd laid her down on the bed. Or the exquisite gentleness with which he'd gathered her into his arms and made love to her a second time, touching her in ways that had made her shiver. She especially remembered the way he'd laughed afterward when she'd confessed she'd always thought men had to wait awhile to "recover" between sexual acts. "Not all men. Not all the time," he'd murmured. "And definitely not me with you." His mouth had found her breast, making her moan as he'd set to proving the truth of his words all over again.

That night had been a revelation—in more ways than one.

After all the years of always holding herself back, of trying to prove that she was a worthwhile person even if she was a Dodd, she'd finally let go. And what she'd found was that with Riley, she was capable of the kind of passion that previously she'd only imagined. She'd given as much as she'd taken, making up in enthusiasm and a surprising lack of inhibition what she'd lacked in experience.

When she'd finally fallen asleep near dawn, deliciously exhausted, her heart had been full. She'd genuinely believed that in Riley's arms she'd found the place she belonged.

When she'd opened her eyes several hours later, he'd been gone.

At first she hadn't been too concerned. She'd told herself he'd probably been late for work, that it had been chivalry that had stopped him from waking her and that he hadn't left her a note because he intended to call her later.

She'd been secure in her belief that what had happened between them had been special, that two people couldn't experience the kind of intimacy they had without sharing a true connection. And so she'd showered and dressed, changed the sheets on the bed—and waited.

For a call that never came. Not that day, or the next, or the one after that.

And still she'd made excuses. Something had happened to him; he'd been in an accident and was lying unconscious in a hospital somewhere. There'd been a work-related emergency, and he'd had to go out of town. She'd spun dozens of outlandish scenarios, ignoring the little voice of reason that told her, among other things, that she would have heard

if he'd been injured and that anywhere he had to go
on Fortune business was bound to have a telephone.

Even her faith had its limits, however, and finally
she'd had to know. Chagrined to realize she didn't
have his home telephone number, which was un-
listed, she'd screwed up her courage and called his
office, braced for the bad news she expected to hear.
Instead, when she asked the receptionist for him, the
woman blandly responded, "One moment, please,
and I'll connect you."

Seconds later, he'd answered. "Riley Fortune."
His voice had been strong, brusque, businesslike and
he'd obviously been hale and hearty. "Hello?"

Feeling as if she'd been punched in the heart,
she'd hung up without a word, all of her illusions
ripped away as she finally accepted that she'd been
deluding herself. What had been the most incredible
experience of her life had been nothing more to him
than a one-night stand.

And oh, how it had hurt.

She was over that now, of course. Over *him.* True,
as she'd proved when he'd shown up without warning at the Corral last week, there were still times
when the memory of how naive and foolish she'd
been hurt. But it wasn't because she was in love
with him. Or because she harbored a silly idea that
some day he'd realize she was the only one for him.
She'd put all those unrealistic dreams behind her.
The only reason she'd married him was because it
was in their baby's best interest.

Which was why tonight just proved that she'd
made the right decision about not sleeping with him.

Because if just being under the same roof with Riley could resurrect the dream of their one night together—and all the feelings it conjured up—she hated to think what would happen if she ever allowed herself to make love to him again.

She'd be lost, his to do with as he wished—while he just skated along in full control, as cool as you please.

It would be a cold day in hell before she allowed that to happen. Riley had some nerve thinking that after three months he could show up without a word, slip a ring on her finger and she'd simply fall into his arms.

Feeling calm and more convinced than ever that she'd made the right decision, however difficult, she headed back toward the house and her solitary bed.

She'd manage. She was nobody's charity case.

Five

"Hi. Is Angelica home?"

Riley considered the young man standing at his front door. The stranger was tall, blond and wholesome looking—and not a day over twenty-one. He was also staring at Riley with an expression that was less than friendly.

Riley propped a shoulder against the jamb and casually crossed his arms. "Yeah, she is. Can I tell her who's asking for her?"

"Chris Rogers. She's expecting me."

"She is, huh?"

"Yeah."

Riley supposed it was possible. Conversation had been a little strained between him and his bride ever since the previous day when she'd dropped her little bombshell about abstaining from sex.

Not that he hadn't been a perfect gentleman. He had. He'd been civil if not exactly enthusiastic when she'd chosen one of the spare bedrooms for herself. He'd remained polite when she'd turned down his invitation to go out to dinner and opted for pizza delivery instead. He'd refrained from making a rude comment when she'd announced she was going to bed—alone—at 8:30. Hell, he'd even managed to stay put later when the alarm on the security pad in his bedroom had gone off shortly after midnight and he'd looked out to see her standing on the patio, the silvery highlights in her hair gleaming in the moonlight.

On second thought, change that from gentleman to saint.

He regarded Junior a little less tolerantly. "The last time I checked, my wife—" he couldn't contain a faint note of irony "—was in the shower. But if you want to leave a message—"

"Riley? I thought you were going to the office." The faint sound of bare feet against the floor tile and the sudden, heady scent of shampoo and clean skin, as much as the sound of her voice, announced Angelica's approach. "Is someone— Mo-mo!" she exclaimed happily.

Riley belatedly shifted his attention to the big dog that had been lolling listlessly at Rogers's feet. On some level he supposed he'd known that Angelica had a pet; the beast had been snoozing off in a corner both times he'd been to her place.

But this was the first time he'd really taken a good look at it, and it wasn't a pretty picture. The animal had big floppy ears, a shaggy coat, a long wiry tail with an unexpected white tip, and it was missing one eye. Adding to its shocking lack of charm, it was the color of dirt and the size of a compact car.

At the sound of the new Mrs. Fortune's voice, the beast dramatically perked up. With something that looked like a smile, the animal gave a woof, leapt up and bounded into the house, its whipcord tail beating the air like a hyperactive metronome.

Angelica laughed and stooped to give the dog a hug, telling him how much she'd missed him in a soft, husky voice that made Riley's pulse pick up. When she finally straightened, however, it wasn't her husband but her visitor who got her attention. "Christopher, hi!" she said warmly. "I see you found the place."

Color suffused Rogers's face and Riley almost felt sorry for the younger man—until he stopped to reflect that it had been three months since Angelica had smiled at *him* that way.

"Yeah. I only got lost twice." The kid made a comical face. "All these mansions look alike."

Angelica made a sympathetic sound. "I know. Did everything else go all right? Did Cosmo behave?"

"Pretty much. Except that he flatly refused to go jogging with me this morning."

Riley suppressed an appreciative grunt. Apparently the dog was smarter than he looked.

"He's not real big on unnecessary exercise," Angelica confided wryly. "Are you, baby?" She gave Cosmo another pat and the dog thumped his tail against the floor, leaving a smattering of dun-colored hairs on the expensive Oriental rug. She again turned her gaze on Rogers. "Did you meet Riley?"

"I know who he is," Rogers replied at the same time that Riley murmured, "Not really."

She glanced between the two of them, her expression puzzled, then seemed to decide her best course of action was to ignore their obvious lack of enthusiasm for each other. She smiled brightly at her guest. "Well, good. I really appreciate you taking care of Cosmo, Chris."

"I brought you a copy of my notes from yesterday." Clearly intent on heading off a dismissal, he pulled a sheaf of papers out of his back pocket. "Lambaugh went over most of the material for the final. I thought you'd want to see it."

"Oh. That's great!" She reached out and gave his arm a squeeze, and to his shock Riley realized he didn't like seeing her touch the other man. Thankfully, his feelings must not have shown, or at least she gave no sign of it as she turned to him and said, "Chris is my study partner. We're both students at the U of A at Tucson."

"You're going to college?"

She laughed self-consciously. "Actually, if I pass all my finals this month, I'll be done. Finally."

Damned if she wasn't full of surprises. Questions crowded his mind, but he wasn't about to expose his ignorance with Junior standing there. "Ah."

The kid didn't have any such reservations. "Are we still on for Thursday?" he asked, pointedly ignoring Riley and stepping closer to Angelica.

"Oh." She frowned. "I don't know."

"What happens Thursday?" Riley inquired.

"That's our usual study night. We've been meeting at my place, but obviously that's no longer an option."

"So meet here."

"Really?"

"Sure. You don't have to ask permission, Angel. This is your home now."

Their eyes met. Hers held surprise and gratitude, and it made him feel funny. Sort of good and guilty all at the same time, since he hadn't offered out of the kindness of his heart, but because he didn't particularly want Junior drooling on her somewhere out of his line of sight.

With a faint shock, he realized that some misguided person might actually accuse him of being...jealous. Not that he was. But still...the mere idea made him feel queasy. He glanced pointedly at his watch. "I'd better get going," he said gruffly. *Before I do or say something I know I'll regret.*

Angelica considered him, a faintly puzzled look on her face. "How long will you be?"

He hiked a shoulder. "Don't know. I'll call you later. If you need me before that, I left the office number on the kitchen counter."

"Okay."

He forced himself to walk away, wondering as he did what was the matter with him. It wasn't as if he and Angelica were in love or anything. So why did having some young pup hanging around her bother him?

But deep down, he knew. Just as he'd realized yesterday, he was never going to be completely at ease with her until he could stop obsessing over the night they'd spent together. While he wouldn't go so far as to say the things he'd felt that night haunted him, he was more than ready to prove to himself that the tenderness and protectiveness, the possessiveness and the hunger, had been merely an aberration. And the only way to do *that* was for him to sleep with her a second time and finally get it out of his system.

Which would be all fine and dandy except that Angelica had made it clear she didn't intend to go along with what he had in mind.

So? Since when have you ever backed off from a challenge? Particularly when it involved a woman. Not that a woman has ever rejected you before, but that's beside the point... If you really think taking Angelica to bed is the right thing to do, don't you owe it to both of you to see it through?

Well...yeah. And not just for his sake, but Angelica's, too, since he'd be a whole lot easier to live with once he was no longer plagued by all these unsettling thoughts.

For everyone's peace of mind, he was just going to have to seduce his wife.

Angelica swallowed a bite of moist, tender chicken and gazed consideringly at Riley, seated across from her at the dining room table. "I have to admit, I never pictured you as knowing your way around the kitchen. But this is delicious."

He took a sip of his wine, his smokey eyes impossible to read in the soft glow of the candlelight. "I have lots of hidden talents. Being able to cook is just one of them."

She didn't doubt that for a minute. They'd been married barely more than twenty-four hours, but she'd be the first to concede that he was just full of surprises.

His house was a case in point. She'd expected it to be beautiful, which it was. But it was also homey and comfortable, and it was clear, from its over-stuffed, pillow-strewn furniture to its well-stocked pantry to its extensive collection of books and CDs that it was Riley's haven. Yet he'd been extremely gracious, telling her it was her house now, too, and she was free to make changes.

His generosity had caught her off guard. So had the mature way he'd accepted her decision to forego making love. While she was still convinced that she'd made the right decision, she had to admit she hadn't expected him to be so understanding. Much less to come home the way he had earlier and announce he intended to cook her dinner.

His graciousness made her feel a little guilty. Not that she regretted her decision to abstain from sex. Or wished he'd put up more of a fuss. But he was being so nice, that it didn't feel right not to reciprocate...

"I don't think I thanked you this morning," she said, taking a bite of her salad.

"For what?"

"For being so understanding about my needing a place to study."

He dismissed his actions with a graceful wave of his hand. "It's no big deal. Although, I was thinking…"

She looked at him warily. "What?"

"Just that you might want to take a leave of absence from your job. That way you could concentrate on school for the next few weeks."

"Oh." It wasn't what she'd expected. "That's a nice idea. Unfortunately, I'm pretty sure the management of the Corral has never heard the term 'leave of absence.' You either work for them or you don't. And even if they had, I need the money."

"Angelica, come on. I have enough for both of us, and if there's anything you want or need, all you have to do is say so. Or if you're not comfortable with that, I'll set up an account for you that's all your own. Whatever you want. Trust me."

There he went again, being kind. And the worst of it was, she was actually tempted to take him up on his generous offer. Thanks to her pregnancy and the emotional turmoil of the past few months, she was tired. It would be nice not to work, to let someone look out for her for a change. And yet…

"I don't know, Riley. Maybe it was the way I grew up, but when someone says trust me, that's the last thing I'm inclined to do."

To her surprise, instead of taking offense, he gave her a slow, wicked grin. "Okay, forget trust me. But you can trust this." His voice altered subtly, getting a little deeper, the cadence slowing. "I'll take real good care of you. I promise."

The words were perfectly innocent, the offer endearing, at least on the surface. But that voice... To her chagrin she was suddenly thinking about skilled fingers and satin sheets. Shifting restlessly on her chair, she told herself not to be foolish. "I'll think about it, okay?"

"Sure." He let it go as easy as that and took another sip of his wine. "What's your major, anyway?"

"Sociology and child psych."

He leaned forward and studied her with obvious interest. "What do you want to do with it?"

"I'd like to do outreach work with disadvantaged kids."

"Like you were?"

"Yes, I suppose."

"I see." The way he said it made her think he really did, that he understood her desire to help children growing up the way she had. But before she could decide how she felt about it, he surprised her anew. "You do realize poor kids aren't the only ones with problems, I hope."

His expression was mild, but there was suddenly something oddly guarded in the depths of his clear gray eyes. "Yes, of course. But poverty creates its own unique set of problems."

He inclined his head. "I'm sure it does. But having money doesn't solve everything, either. There's a lot of pressure to measure up, to always do the right thing."

She considered him, realizing with a faint shock that he was talking about himself. Not sure what to say, and sensing from the way he was suddenly twisting his wineglass in his fingers that he was already regretting the extent to which he'd revealed himself, she made an impulsive decision to switch gears. "Did your sister-in-law get ahold of you? She called here earlier, and I told her you were at the office."

"Cynthia?" His fingers stilled. "Yeah. We talked."

"Is everything all right?"

"Why wouldn't it be?"

"I don't know. I just thought... Isn't she your attorney?"

"Yeah."

"Has there been news about your case?"

"If you mean, has she made like Perry Mason and found the person who's really to blame for your brother's death and cleared my name yet, the answer is no."

Despite his nonchalant tone, there was something in the set of his chin, the sudden tautness around his mouth that suggested he wasn't nearly as unconcerned about the subject as he wanted her to believe. Not that it surprised her. As she'd already realized, there was more to Riley than simply a great body and a handsome face.

For half a second she actually considered telling him what she suspected about Mike, but she swiftly caught herself. After all, she didn't have proof that her brother had actually been involved in any wrongdoing, only a feeling. And even if she discovered something in the future, it might not prove to have any bearing on his murder. The last thing she wanted was to give Riley false hopes.

On the other hand, she felt a renewed urgency to go through Mike's things—no matter how painful it might be. After all, Riley was her baby's father. Despite their ongoing differences, she didn't want him to go to prison. Or for their child to grow up thinking its father was a murderer.

Suddenly aware that she'd been silent too long, she said abruptly, "I'm sorry."

He shrugged. "There's no reason for you to be." There was an awkward silence that ended as he pushed back his chair and stretched out his legs. "I dropped by my folks earlier."

"Oh. Did you tell them about us?"

"Mm-hmm."

"What did they say?"

"At first, they were…surprised. But then when I explained about the pregnancy, they understood."

Angelica could just imagine what his parents "understood." Not knowing what to say, she took a sip of milk from her glass, grateful as Cosmo suddenly lumbered into sight.

The big shaggy dog gave her a brief look, but chose Riley for his main target, crowding close and staring at him with a pitiful look that said clearly, "Feed me, please, I'm starving."

Riley considered the dog's hopeful countenance, then glanced uncertainly at Angelica. "Didn't he like the dog food I bought him?"

"Oh, I think he did," she said dryly. "He licked the bowl clean. The sad truth is he'll eat anything, much less an expensive gourmet brand."

"Ah." Riley reconsidered the beast. "So he's just looking for a patsy?"

"Right."

"Hey, I can do that." Taking her by surprise, he broke off a chunk of chicken. Before she could protest, he offered it to the dog, which promptly wolfed it down in a single bite.

"Riley, don't! He's not supposed to beg at the table. And you're not supposed to feed him."

"Even if I just made a friend for life?"

"Yes." It was a struggle to look stern. "Although I suppose I can forgive you, since you're being so nice about having him here."

"I like dogs."

"Even if they don't exactly go with your decor?"

"Even then." He drained the last of his wine and set his beautifully etched crystal goblet back on the table. "Houses are meant to be lived in. And unlike the dog I had as a kid, he seems like a pretty mellow guy. He should be fine with the baby."

She pictured him as a little boy, and not too surprisingly was instantly charmed. "You had a dog?"

"Sure. His name was Jake."

Intrigued, she asked, "What happened to him?"

"We had to get rid of him after my sister Isabelle was born. He was big and sort of hyper, and when she started to walk he was always knocking her down and jumping on her, which didn't go over too well with my mother."

"That must've been hard."

He negligently hitched a shoulder. "I survived. And it was probably for the best. I was a real trial to my folks, always getting into trouble. Without Jake around, I spent more time with my brother, who they always considered a civilizing influence."

Out of nowhere, she had the oddest urge to reach over, push back the inky strand of hair that fell over his forehead and comfort him somehow. Which was utterly ridiculous. She'd never known a person more capable of taking care of himself than Riley Fortune.

A point that was driven home as his mouth suddenly tipped up in an impish grin. "Though I've got to admit, if it'd been left up to me, I would've voted to get rid of Isabelle."

She felt that smile clear to her toes and couldn't help but respond with one of her own. "Somehow that doesn't surprise me."

Their eyes met. After a few seconds, his dark lashes drooped a fraction, giving him a heavy-lidded look that was all male.

She flushed as she realized she was squeezing her thighs together in reaction. "Well." She forced herself to look away from him, pushed back her chair and grabbed her plate. "I'd better get started on these dishes."

He stood. "I'll help."

It was the last thing she wanted. "That's all right. I can take care of it."

"I insist." His fingers grazed hers as they both reached for the basket of rolls. "I like to finish what I start."

Why did that sound more like a threat than a simple declaration? she wondered as she snatched back her tingling hand and hurried toward the kitchen. "If you say so." Biting her lip, she told herself to get a grip.

It was easier said than done. She heard him approach, then froze as he leaned around her to set the basket on the counter. The heat of his body enveloped her; so did his scent. She fought the urge to just let go and melt against him. "Riley?"

"Hmm?" He braced his hand and leaned even closer, his face so intent as he gazed down at her that she was sure he was going to kiss her.

"If you really don't mind about the dishes—" she ducked her head and scooted to safety beneath his arm "—I think I'll go study."

He slowly straightened. For a second she thought she saw a hint of frustration flash across his face, but then it was gone. But all he said was, "No problem."

She didn't wait around to see if he changed his mind.

Six

"Angelica?" Riley strode through the quiet house, wondering where his wife was.

He'd already checked the bedrooms, the pool, the living and family rooms, to no avail. He supposed she might have gone for a walk, although with Cosmo asleep behind the chair in the family room as usual it seemed unlikely. That left the possibility that she'd driven somewhere. Walking past the utility room, he opened the door to the garage to check.

A wave of warm, stuffy air, and the sight of her car, greeted him. For a moment he was perplexed, and then a movement to his left caught his eye. Looking over to where he'd had the overflow of her belongings stacked, he spotted her seated cross-legged on the concrete floor. Next to her was an open box and several stacks of papers. "There you are."

She looked up, her cheeks flushed from the heat that lay over the room like a blanket. "Riley."

"What are you doing?"

She hesitated, a flash of something almost furtive crossing her face. "Looking for some class notes."

"Any luck?"

"Not yet."

"You don't have to sort through this stuff out here, you know. If you show me which boxes you want to go through, I'll be happy to move them into one of the spare bedrooms later."

Inexplicably, she hesitated again before nodding. "Thanks. That'd be nice." Her gazed raked over him, a frown creasing her brow as she took in his fresh slacks and black polo shirt. "I thought you were going to play racquetball this morning."

"I did." Never one for organized sport, he'd discovered a few years ago that the game was a great way to burn off his aggressions and keep in shape. "I showered and changed at the club afterward."

"Oh. So how was it? The game, I mean?"

"Fine. Rowan's not nearly as good as he thinks he is."

"Rowan?"

"Brad Rowan. Isabelle's fiancé. My opponent."

A frown marred her brow. "You don't like him?"

He stared at her, surprised by her insight. Not that he had any intention of admitting he had reservations about his sister's intended. Much less confiding that he wished he felt better about Isabelle's reasons for getting married in the first place. Baring his soul wasn't his style. And even if it had been, now definitely wasn't the time. "He's okay. It doesn't really matter what I think as long as he makes my sister happy. Speaking of my family, we have company."

"We do? Who?"

"My mother. She drove in right after I did and informed me she wants to meet you."

"Your mother's *here?*" She scrambled to her feet, trying—and failing—to mask her dismay.

"I know it's lousy timing—"

"Do you think?" She reached down to tug at the hem of her shorts. "Or are you just now noticing that I'm not exactly dressed for company."

She had a point. She *was* a little dusty. And her baby blue tank top, navy shorts and rubber flip-flops were definitely on the casual side. On the other hand, it wasn't as if she were naked or anything. And since his mother wasn't about to leave, they really didn't have a choice except to make the best of it—and be damned grateful his dad was playing golf and hadn't come, too.

He cleared his throat. "Try to relax. My mother's a lot more interested in who you are than what you're wearing."

"Oh, that's reassuring," she murmured, scooping up the papers scattered around her and dumping them back in the box. Dusting her hands on her shorts, she straightened her spine and walked toward him, her lips pursed.

He stepped back to give her some room, feeling a strange combination of sympathy for her anxiety and admiration for her willingness to see it through anyway.

And then she brushed past him and a third, more elemental emotion came over him as her bare arm rubbed against his. He jerked back, annoyed by his inability to stop the prickle of desire that sliced through him at even that innocent touch.

His annoyance didn't improve as he found himself following her down the hallway, with nowhere to look except at her bare, slender legs, shapely fanny and the tops of her golden-skinned shoulder blades.

It should have been a relief to reach the family room. And it would have been, if not for the sight that greeted him.

His mother was seated on the couch where he'd left her, looking less than thrilled as Cosmo pressed up against her, his front feet planted on the sofa cushion, his tail wagging happily as he energetically sniffed the front of her elegant lavender pantsuit. "It appears you've acquired a pet." Although she managed a smile, her voice was strained.

Angelica sucked in a horrified breath. "Cosmo, no! Get down, right now."

To his credit, the dog instantly obeyed. Backing away, he sent a shamed look his mistress's way that left no doubt he knew he'd misbehaved and slunk sheepishly toward his place behind the chair. So great was his contrition that it would've been funny if not for Angelica's distress.

"I'm so sorry," she said fervently, her eyes dark with anxiety as she addressed his mother. "I can't imagine what got into him. He's usually much better behaved.''

Riley laid a steadying hand on her shoulder. "It's okay. Mom's tougher than she looks.''

Both women sliced him looks; Angelica's was unconvinced, his mother's first reproachful, then thoughtful as her gaze slid from his face to his hand—and finally to his wife. "Riley's right. After all, I survived raising him, which was no small feat.''

"Some countries give medals of bravery for less,'' he said, only half-kidding. "Mom, this is Angelica. Angelica, my mother, Joan.''

His mother inclined her head. "Hello, Angelica.''

"It's nice to meet you, Mrs. Fortune.'' Angelica tried, but she suspected her smile was strained at best. Although she knew she was overreacting, seeing Riley and his mother together, both so polished and good-looking, and hearing them banter in a way that would've been unimaginable in the household she'd grown up in, made her feel awkward and out of place, like the trailer park kid she'd been.

"Call me Joan, please. I apologize for dropping in unannounced this way, but I didn't want to wait another day to welcome you to the family.''

More likely to check her out, Angelica found herself thinking. Not that she blamed the older woman. Although the Fortunes were known for their family loyalty, she strongly doubted she was what this stylish woman had envisioned for a daughter-in-law. "That's very kind of you,'' she managed, giving a little jump of surprise as Riley nudged her toward one of the club chairs, then lowered himself onto the matching ottoman.

She sat and tried to relax, not easy given the situation and his proximity.

"We were all very sorry about your brother," Joan said quietly.

"Thank you."

"Are you getting settled in?"

"Yes. I was just doing some unpacking." She regretted the words the instant she said them, since they sounded exactly like what they were: an apology for her grubby attire.

Riley's mother didn't seem to notice. Instead, a faint frown creased her brow. "I do hope you weren't moving anything heavy. You have to take care of yourself, you know."

In your condition. Joan may not have said the words out loud, but Angelica got the picture. She drew herself up a little taller. "I wouldn't do anything to hurt the baby."

"Of course not," the other woman said quickly.

You wouldn't dream of it, since that's the only reason my son married you. Angelica clasped her hands tightly together and told herself fiercely to quit putting words in the other woman's mouth. Yet she couldn't seem to stop the tension coiling tighter and tighter inside her.

There was an awkward silence. "Frankly, I've always thought this house was made for a family," Joan said brightly. "Although—" she shifted her gaze to Riley "—I do hope you know you're going to have to fence off the pool. It's not safe for a child the way it is."

"Don't worry, Mom," he said easily. "We've got some time. I'll get it taken care of."

Joan face softened. "I'm sure you will. As I'm sure you'll discover when you get to know him better—" although addressing Angelica she kept her gaze on her offspring "—my son is actually quite a homebody. Despite what he wants everyone to think."

"Damn." Riley's voice held mock despair. "There goes my reputation."

"You know it's true, sweetheart," Joan replied serenely. "Not that you don't have your faults." Her voice turned a tad brusque. "Did you remember to tell Angelica about the shower?"

He shook his head. "Nope. Sorry. I forgot."

"I thought as much." Unperturbed, Joan turned to Angelica. "Isabelle is getting married at the end of the month. Cynthia is having a wedding shower for her next Thursday, and as the newest member of the family, you simply must come. Everyone will want to meet you."

Just the thought of being an object of interest to an entire room of Fortunes made Angelica feel shaky. She needed some time to get accustomed to this marriage herself before she went public—particularly in that company. She took a deep breath. "That's very kind of you, but I'm afraid I can't."

"Oh." His mother was clearly taken aback.

"I—I've already got plans for that night. I'm sorry."

She felt Riley turn and stare at her, but before she could screw up the courage to meet his gaze and gauge his reaction, he turned back to his mother. "Like I told you, Mom, Angelica's finishing up at the university. Thursday is her usual study night, but I'm sure she can change her plans. At the very least, she can try. Right, Angel?"

Stunned by his nerve, she wanted in the worst way to say no. But then she caught herself. After all, she wasn't trying to insult Joan Fortune, just give herself some breathing room. And saying she would try wasn't the same as actually agreeing to go. Something she intended to explain to her husband the instant they were alone. "Yes, of course."

"Good." Riley smiled at his mother. "We'll get it figured out and call you."

"That's fine." Nobody's fool, Joan was clearly aware of the tension in the room, but her pleasant expression didn't change. "And now I'd better be going. Your father and I are due for bridge at the Bennett's in about an hour. Angelica, it's been nice to meet you."

"You, too, Mrs. Fortune."

Riley came smoothly to his feet. "I'll walk you out."

Angelica's shoulders sagged with relief as the pair exited the room. Worn out by the strain of the conversation, she leaned back in the chair and tried to calm her over-taxed nerves.

It was easier said than done, particularly when Riley reentered the room. Coming to a halt by the couch, he fixed her with a level stare. "You want to tell me what that was all about?" he demanded.

She met his look with one of her own. "I'd be glad to—right after you apologize for that little end run you did around me."

His eyebrows shot up in disbelief. "My mother goes out of her way to invite you to a family function, you blow her off and *you* think *I* owe you an apology?"

"Yes."

He kept an admirable hold on his temper. "All right. Maybe I shouldn't have done that. But dammit, Angelica, you hurt my mother's feelings!"

"I'm sorry," she said stiffly. "I certainly didn't mean to be rude."

"Well, you were. Isabelle isn't just the only girl in the family, she's the baby. And since Shane and I both opted for something other than a big church wedding, my mom's going all out. This means a lot to her."

"I didn't realize."

"Then you'll go?"

"No!"

"Why not?"

"For all sorts of reasons."

"Name one."

I don't want to. I wouldn't belong. I wouldn't know how to act. She pursed her lips, pride refusing to let her give voice to the thoughts running through her head. Yet she had to say something... "I don't have a thing to wear."

Her pronouncement was met with a thunderous silence. "That's it? *That's* the problem?"

Chagrined—why couldn't she have come up with something that sounded less shallow?—she nodded. "Part of it."

"That's easy to fix. Go shopping."

"No."

"Why not? If it's the money—"

"No, that's not it," she said quickly. "I just...I wouldn't know where to go. Or what to get. Believe it or not, the places where I usually shop don't have a designer section." She raised her chin, daring him to comment.

He was silent for the space of a heartbeat. And then to her dismay, something in his expression changed from annoyed to thoughtful. "Okay. Then I'll take you."

"What?"

"We can go today."

"No!"

"Why not?"

"Because..." *I'm nobody's charity case. And the last thing I want is to feel beholden to you. Much less when it involves spending an afternoon taking off my clothes in front of you!* Yet there was no way—no way—she could say that and she knew it. She swallowed. "I need a shower."

"So take one. I need to make a few phone calls anyway."

They stared at each other. Her heart skipped a beat as she realized that along with everything else, she'd neatly trapped herself into spending time with him.

And she could see, by the sudden gleam in his eyes that Riley knew it, too.

"Where are we going?" Angelica asked as Riley guided the Corvette past the gatehouse at the entrance to Saguaro Springs and turned toward town.

"I called my sister. She gave me a list of places where she shops. She usually looks okay, so I thought it would be a place to start."

Isabelle Fortune looked "okay"? It was the sort of statement only a brother could make. Still, with more than a little chagrin Angelica found she was relieved that he didn't seem to be accustomed to buying clothes for women.

Way to go, girl. Married to a man who doesn't love you and you're feeling territorial.

It was hardly a reassuring thought. She tried to tell herself it meant nothing, only to realize she was lying a moment later when she found herself taking advantage of Riley's concentration on his driving to admire his profile. She made herself look away. Yet she couldn't seem to get his image out of her mind: silky black hair, thickly lashed eyes, strong nose, chiseled lips. Worse, she kept remembering the moment earlier in the family room when his expression had changed, and she'd had the disconcerting sense that he'd seen beneath the surface to what she was really feeling.

The short drive to town seemed to take forever. Maneuvering through the light weekend traffic, Riley swung the car into a parking spot in front of a shop in Pueblo's most exclusive shopping district. An ultra-fashionable black-and-white suit was displayed in the window, while a discreet sign hanging above the door read Los Palmas.

"You ready?" Riley opened his door.

"I suppose."

"Let's go, then."

A bell tinkled discreetly as they entered the shop. An attractive woman standing behind a curved counter looked up. Covering the receiver of the phone pressed to her ear, she said pleasantly, "Hi. I'll be right with you."

Riley nodded and she went back to her conversation.

Angelica looked around. The shop's interior was warm and cozy. The air smelled faintly of vanilla, while the peach-toned carpet felt thick and plush beneath her feet. There were a number of attractive displays, including one where a rainbow of sheer, delicate scarves were draped artfully over a spoke-back chair. Entranced, she crossed over to take a closer look, only to stop at a circular stand holding coats, skirts and slacks in a mouth-watering array of pastels. Running her fingertips over a silky sage-green jacket, she glanced at the price tag, and nearly fainted. She took a hasty step back—and bumped smack into Riley's warm, solid frame.

His breath tickled her temple as his arm came up to steady her. "What's the matter?"

She turned to face him. "Do you have any idea what things cost here?"

His gaze played over her face, then he reached around her, took a quick glance at the tag attached to a pair of pants, and straightened. "So?" He swept a tendril of her hair over her shoulder, his fingers grazing her neck.

With that single touch, her shock over the prices evaporated as all of her senses responded to him. She could feel the heat from his skin, see the shadow of the beard beneath his cheeks, hear the even ebb and flow of his every breath, smell his intoxicating scent. She struggled to remember what they were talking about. "It's too much."

"Oh, I don't know." His mouth curved in an enigmatic smile. "I think you're worth it."

There was no safe way to respond to that. Fighting a desire to lean forward and press her face against the smooth V of skin exposed by his open collar, she forced herself to look away, desperate for a diversion. "Oh. A sales rack." It wasn't much but it would do. She took a step away.

His fingers closed around her wrist. "Wait."

The contact jolted through her. "What?"

"Just...don't worry about prices, okay? Pick out what you like, and we'll figure out the rest of it later."

She opened her mouth to protest, only to shut it again as the saleswoman walked up. "I'm sorry I kept you waiting," the woman said. "Can I help you find something?"

"No," Angelica answered in the same breath that Riley said, "Yes. My wife needs something to wear to a wedding shower."

"Do you have a preference for dresses or slacks?"

"Dresses," Riley answered at the same time Angelica said "Pants."

Discreet amusement blossomed in the saleslady's eyes. She glanced back and forth between them, then settled her gaze on Riley and smiled warmly. "Perhaps I could show you both?"

"That'd be fine. We can start with this." He indicated the jacket Angelica had been looking at moments earlier.

"Oh, good choice. This comes with both a skirt and slacks." She looked Angelica over as she fanned through the rack. "Size eight?"

"Yes."

Quickly selecting a handful of items, the woman returned her gaze to Riley. "Is there anything else in particular you'd like to see?"

"Yeah. How about that?" He indicated one of the display dresses, a sleeveless sheath that came with a short cashmere jacket, both in a luscious melon color with subtle beading at the hem and neck.

In what seemed like no time, he and the saleslady had settled on half a dozen other outfits. Angelica found herself closeted in one of the two spacious dressing rooms at the back of the shop.

Feeling a little dazed as she stared at all the beautiful clothing they'd selected, she took a deep breath and slowly stepped out of her sandals, unzipped her blue-and-green floral wrap skirt and unbuttoned her sleeveless white blouse. She folded them and set them on the plush chair in the corner, and, after a momentary hesitation, reached for an apricot-colored pantsuit.

She slipped into the pants and top, not sure whether she felt relieved or disappointed as she found that the color was all wrong for her. Taking the outfit off, she hung it back on the hanger and in quick succession tried on two more ensembles, one white with mother of pearl buttons, the other a soft shade of lavender. Both fit well and looked great. Unable to decide which one she liked better, she set them aside and reached for the melon-colored dress.

She carefully slid the finely-woven fabric over her head and twisted pretzel-like to zip it. Turning back around, she stepped into her medium-heeled sandals and faced the mirror, a little taken aback at her image. The dress fit as if made for her, the rich color the perfect foil for her silvery brown hair. She touched one of the delicate beaded flowers along the neckline, a little awed at how pretty the effect was.

A familiar voice interrupted her reverie. "Angelica? How's it going in there?"

She cracked the door and peeked out. Riley was seated on a low velvet banquette, his long legs stretched out before him. Another man might have looked silly or uncomfortable in such feminine surroundings; he just looked bigger and more blatantly male.

He looked at her inquiringly. "Well? Do I get to see or not?"

Not, the wiser part of her thought in the same instant that its more reckless counterpart said, "Sure." Committed, she stepped gingerly into the waiting area, pointedly not looking at the three-way mirror mounted on the opposite wall.

Riley stood, and walked slowly around her. "I like it," he said finally. "That's a terrific color on you. What do you think?"

What she thought was that it was an I-feel-beautiful dress and that she loved it. But she was also very aware that she hadn't yet had the courage to look at the price tag. Reluctant to sound too enthusiastic until she had, she took a firm rein on her emotions. "It's pretty."

"It's more than that." Before she could stop him, he stepped behind her and turned her to face the mirror. Gathering her hair into his hands, he smoothed it down her back, combing it with his fingers, before resting his palms on her shoulders. "It's perfect."

Angelica's breath caught. Not at her hair, or herself in the dress, but at the sight of the two of them together. She seemed to glow in the warmly-colored fabric, while Riley looked cool and austere in a pale gray shirt and slim gray slacks. His body framed hers, bigger, stronger, darker. The contrast between them made her think of sunshine and shadow, intrinsically linked, meant to be together.

His gaze met hers in the mirror. "Beautiful," he murmured.

She knew he didn't mean the dress. Transfixed, she watched as he slid his tanned hands slowly down her paler arms, her lips parting at the delicious warmth of his palms. Wrapping his fingers around the soft skin above her elbows, he stepped closer, the heat from his body a brand against her back. Her eyelids suddenly felt heavy, and yet she couldn't quit watching as he bent his head toward her, slid a hand beneath her hair to rest against her nape and brushed his lips over the hypersensitive spot where her neck met the point of her jaw.

Pleasure erupted. Her stomach somersaulted. As if watching someone else, she saw her head droop to the side, giving him better access, while she reached up to cup the strong, silky line of his jaw in her palm. Then she saw nothing as she closed her eyes and angled her head sideways, seeking his lips—

"Is everything going all right?" the saleslady inquired a second before she swept into the dressing area.

Startled, Angelica snapped her head up and spun sideways, out of Riley's arms. Heat rising in her cheeks, she plastered a smile on her face, operating on instinct alone. "Everything's fine."

The world's biggest lie. Given another twenty-five seconds alone with Riley, who knew what she might have done?

Blissfully ignorant of her inner turmoil, the saleslady beamed. "Oh, my, I should say so. That dress looks wonderful on you." She shifted her gaze to Riley. "Don't you agree?"

He glanced sideways at Angelica, and she felt his hooded gaze like a heated touch. "Oh, yeah."

"Have you tried the jacket on yet?" the saleslady innocently inquired.

"No, not yet."

"You really should. Just to make sure it fits, since the dress seems to be made for you."

"Yes, of course." Excessively grateful for any excuse to escape, Angelica took a step toward the dressing room, only to rock to a stop as Riley got there before her, blocking the doorway.

"I'll get it." He ducked inside. Emerging with the garment seconds later, he blandly addressed the saleslady. "You wouldn't happen to have any suggestions for jewelry, would you?"

"Well, yes, of course." Clearly sensing a substantial sale in the works, the woman beamed and hurried back toward the merchandise area. "I'll be right back to show you."

And just like that, they were alone. Again.

"Shall we see how this looks?" Riley held up the jacket, motioning her to try it on, his expression as innocent as a choirboy's.

She pressed her hand to her tingling lips, and stared at him warily. "I'm not sure that's wise."

"Sure it is. But if it makes you feel better, I swear that from now on, I'll be on my best behavior. All you have to do is trust me."

Ah, there were those words again. Only unlike the last time he'd said them to her, this time there was a part of her that wanted to do just that.

Not that she intended to lower her guard completely. But he was clearly making an effort; what could it hurt to try and meet him halfway?

Gingerly, she turned and slipped her arms into the jacket.

"Good choice," Riley murmured, his gaze once more meeting hers in the mirror.

Angelica wished she was half so sure as he was.

Seven

Riley settled the life-size stuffed panda bear on the family room couch. Fluffing the red satin bow that encircled the bear's neck, he pushed an inquisitive Cosmo away and stepped back next to Angelica. Side-by-side, they contemplated his first purchase for their child. "So what do you think?"

It was a moment before she answered. "I think buying a few boxes of diapers would have been a lot more practical." Her attempt to sound stern was ruined by the gleam of amusement in her wide green eyes.

He shrugged, unperturbed. "Maybe. But my guy's going to look a whole lot better in the baby's room."

"Now that, I concede."

"So what do you think we should call him? Pandas in zoos always seem to have two syllable names, Ling-Ling, Yum-Yum, that sort of thing."

She appeared to consider. "How about Boo-Boo?" she finally ventured.

He raised an eyebrow. "Very funny."

Her mouth turned up. "I thought so." After a moment, she sobered. "Riley?"

"Hmm?"

"I had a really nice time today. Thank you for taking me."

"My pleasure." And it had been. Though his body had been humming like a downed electrical wire ever since their close encounter in the Los Palmas dressing room, he'd deliberately pulled back after that and set out to charm her. In addition to doing more shopping, he'd bought her dinner and dessert and entertained her with a few of the funnier stories of his misspent youth. And while his self-imposed restraint had been a strain, at some point he'd realized he was having fun.

"Well." She tucked a loose strand of hair behind her ear. "I guess I'll get started unloading the car—"

"Don't worry about it. I'll take care of it in a little while."

"Gosh, I don't know, Riley." That austere note was back in her voice. "Given the way you insisted on buying out half the town, it'll probably take both of us to haul it all in."

"Now, Angel." He pretended to look hurt. "Don't start that again. You had to have shoes and stuff to go with the clothes. And you can't very well go to the shower without a gift.''

She sighed, but her eyes gave her away, softening as she looked at him. "I suppose you're right.''

"You bet I am.''

Buoyed by that small victory, he looked around and saw that the last rays of the day's sunlight were slanting through the windows. Out of nowhere, he found himself reaching for her hand and tugging her toward the sliding glass door. "Come here. There's something I want you to show you.''

She resisted for all of a second, then gave in, following as he led the way outside toward the far end of the terrace above the pool, where they had a one-hundred-and-eighty degree view of the desert stretched out before them. "Look.''

He directed her gaze to the west, where the sun was sinking toward the horizon. The sky above it was awash in brilliant layers of tangerine and magenta, coral and crimson. And then while they watched, the sun slipped completely away, and for one magic moment, as the sky dimmed to lavender and the first early stars appeared overhead, it was perfectly quiet, as if the world itself were holding its breath.

In the ensuing silence, Riley suddenly felt embarrassed. After all, how stupid was this? Only some mushy-hearted romantic would drag a woman out to watch a sunset—and he was definitely not that. Was he? God help him, but maybe his rampaging hormones were turning his brain to mush—

As if emerging from a spell, Angelica unexpectedly laid her hand on his arm. "Wow. That was really something."

It was the first time since their marriage that she'd voluntarily touched him. Some of the tension drained out of his body. "Yeah."

"Do you know how lucky you are?" she said suddenly. "It's so beautiful and private here. Sometimes I like to just sit in the house and listen to the quiet. It's such a luxury."

There was a wistfulness in her voice that made his throat tighten. Determined to lighten the mood, he said, "Is that your way of telling me you'd like me to quit singing in the shower?"

To his relief, she laughed. The sound bubbled through his veins like champagne. "No. But I would appreciate it if you'd refrain from any more surprises. I think I've reached my limit."

He rocked back on his heels. "What?"

"I just always assumed you were the kind of guy who liked to watch the sun come up," she teased. "Not go down."

"Ah." He turned to look at her. Her face alight, she looked beautiful in the fading twilight. Knowing he was taking a chance, but suddenly feeling reckless, he didn't try to hide his hunger for her. "The truth is, I'm both."

Her expression sobered. "Riley..." It was half protest, half entreaty. "Don't."

Bracing his hands on the rail behind her, he dipped his head. "Why not?"

"You know why."

"No. Not really." Nor did he care, not at this

moment. After all, he'd been a good boy most of the day. And she was too close, too tempting, and he wanted her too much.

He leaned down and found her mouth with his own.

She stiffened for half a second. Then, to his fierce satisfaction, she made a soft little sound of pleasure and her hands came up around his neck. He pulled her closer.

Although an accomplished kisser, Riley had never particularly cared about the act one way or another. It had been a means to an end, an opening move, a prelude to pleasure.

But this…with Angelica…it was different. To his shock, he found himself craving the intimacy of being face-to-face and mouth-to-mouth with her. Her mouth was warm and far sweeter than he remembered, while the press of lips, the tangle of tongues, the melding of breath was unbearably sensual.

He slanted his head and caught her lower lip between his teeth. He applied gentle pressure, then soothed the tiny hurt with his tongue, lost in the taste and feel of her. "Damn," he murmured against her mouth, "but you're sweet…"

He wrapped his arm around her waist. Her hair slid over his forearm in a satiny ripple that made him groan. In a flash of memory, he recalled the night they'd spent together and how he'd fisted his hands in her hair as she'd twisted beneath him…

The delicious softness of warm skin beneath his fingertips jolted him back to the here and now, and he realized her blouse had ridden up. He stroked his palm along the dip in her spine and pulled her closer, feeling as if he could go on kissing her forever.

He might have, too, if she hadn't suddenly drawn back and averted her head. "Riley, stop." Her breasts pressed sweetly against him as she struggled to catch her breath.

"Shh. It's okay," he murmured, taking advantage of her posture to press an open-mouthed kiss to the pulse pounding in her throat.

"No, it's not," she said, her voice a little stronger.

It took him a moment to realize she was making a half-hearted effort to push him away. He lifted his head, puzzled, and took a half step back. "What's the matter?"

"We have to stop."

Deprived of her mouth, he abruptly became aware of the insistent throbbing of his body. "No, we don't."

"Yes, we do." She looked up at him. Her lips were swollen, her cheeks flushed, her eyelids heavy and the hands she raised to push her hair back shook. Yet there was a spark of determination lighting her eyes. "I'm sorry. I let things get out of hand. I shouldn't have."

For the second time in a handful of days, he told himself she had to be kidding. "Angel—"

"I'm sorry," she repeated. "I just…can't." To his disbelief, she stepped away from him and dashed for the house.

He swiveled around to draw her back but she was already out of reach. "Angelica, come back!"

All he got for an answer was a swift shake of her head before she disappeared inside.

Well, hell. With a savage oath, he fought the urge to go after her. After all, he had his pride. And he wasn't sure what he'd say if he did catch up with her. Besides, while it was true he wanted her, she had to be willing.

Around him the landscaping lights kicked on as the night settled into velvety darkness. Face grim, he made a sudden decision. Kicking off his shoes, he stripped out of his clothes and stalked across the terrace, down the stairs and dove into the swimming pool.

The water felt icy cold against his overheated skin. He surfaced, gasping at the shock of it. And yet, as he tossed his head to get the wet hair out of his eyes, his mind felt clear again.

He thought once more about the way she'd taken off. There'd been a sort of desperation to her actions. As if she didn't trust herself to stay. As if she didn't trust herself not to want him.

That was good. So, he realized on further reflection, was the way she'd kissed him, as if she couldn't get enough of him. Sure, she'd managed to rein herself in there at the end, but it had taken a monumental effort. She must want him a whole lot more than she was letting on.

So all in all, it had actually gone pretty well. Sure, he'd suffered a minor setback. But that didn't mean he was giving up. Not by a long shot.

He stubbornly refused to acknowledge the thought that, somewhere along the line, what had begun as mere physical desire was beginning to feel a whole lot like overwhelming need.

The soft clink of ice cubes in crystal punch cups mixed with the low murmur of feminine voices in Cynthia and Shane's elegant living room.

Luncheon had been served; a trio of games played; the shower gifts opened. Now, Angelica listened as the women around her talked about subjects ranging from their jobs to their opinions regarding a recent movie to the best place to buy local produce.

Their clothes might be more expensive and their jokes more subdued, but they weren't really that different from the women she knew at work or those from her old neighborhood, she mused.

The discovery was a revelation, and with sudden insight she realized that in large part she had Riley to thank for it. He'd not only pushed her to come, but he'd made sure that outwardly, at least, she'd fit in. Armed with that exterior measure of confidence, she'd been able to relax enough to see that these women, either Fortunes by birth or marriage, or friends of the family, were simply people like any others.

She absentmindedly smoothed a finger over the silky material of her lavender pantsuit, her thoughts zeroing in on her husband.

She supposed she should be used to it by now, but in the near week since they'd shared that knee-weakening kiss out on the terrace, he'd surprised her. Because of the way things had ended that night, she'd expected him to be cool with her afterward, if not openly angry; instead, he'd been just as charming as ever.

He'd continued to cook dinner, taken Cosmo for walks so she could study, even insisted on driving her back and forth to class. And though she suspected he wasn't quite as sanguine about her rejection as he wanted her to believe—several times she'd caught him watching her with a brooding look on his face—he hadn't forced the issue.

Which raised disturbing questions about his character. Whether it was his intention or not, she was beginning to find it impossible to think of him as a shallow playboy.

Determined not to dwell on it, she forced herself to look around. Across the room, Riley's mother sat on the loveseat near the door, talking to Kate Fortune, the family matriarch. Angelica studied the two for a moment, and felt an unexpected tug of affection. Joan had been wonderful to her today. Acting as if last Saturday's strained conversation had never taken place, she'd taken Angelica around and personally introduced her to everyone, insuring her acceptance by her obvious approval.

As for Kate, the elegant old lady had singled her out at the start of the shower and the two had visited on and off all afternoon.

As if feeling her gaze now, Kate looked directly at her and with an imperious crook of her hand, waved her over. ''Angelica, my dear, would you be

good enough to get me another glass of punch?''
She held out her empty glass.

That'll teach you to get too comfortable. Once a
waitress, always a waitress, she thought with an inner smile. "I'd be glad to. What about you?" she
asked Joan. "Can I get you something?''

"No, thank you. I think I've had more than
enough to eat today," Riley's mother said with a
soft chuckle. "You might see if you can find out
where Cynthia's disappeared to, however. I should
be going but I'd like to say goodbye."

"Sure.'' Angelica threaded her way into where
the buffet was set up in the dining room. Moving to
the punch bowl, she glanced around but their hostess
was nowhere in sight. She looked questioningly at
Julie Parker Fortune, Riley's cousin Tyler's wife,
who was standing on the opposite side of the table,
pouring herself a glass of sparkling water. "Have
you seen Cynthia?''

"I think she's on the phone," the sweet-faced for-
mer librarian, a newlywed herself, answered.

"Thanks.''

Returning to the living room, she saw that Joan
was now standing by the fireplace, visiting with her
sister-in-law. She walked over to report what she'd
discovered, then made her way to the loveseat where
Kate was waiting. She handed the older woman the
cup and sat down beside her.

"Thank you, my dear." Kate took a sip of her
punch, then set the cup down on the end table beside
her. "I trust you've enjoyed your first Fortune family function?''

"Actually, I have."

"You sound surprised."

Angelica smiled a little sheepishly. "I guess I didn't expect everyone to be so nice."

Kate nodded, her expression suddenly thoughtful. "I've lived a fairly long life, and I've found that with a few memorable exceptions, people are much the same everywhere, regardless of their social status."

The sentiment was so close to what Angelica had been thinking earlier that she gave a start. She looked curiously at the other woman. "Am I that transparent?" she asked.

Kate patted her hand. "Only to someone who's really paying attention."

The doorbell rang, interrupting their conversation. One of Isabelle's friends was standing nearest to the front entry. She glanced around. Not seeing Cynthia, she gave a little shrug, walked over and opened the door, stepping back a few seconds later to admit an athletically built man with sandy hair and shrewd hazel eyes.

Angelica felt a tug of recognition, then realized that it was Link Templeton, the investigator who was heading up the inquiry into Mike's death. Her interest piqued, she watched as he took a quick look around, then saw him freeze as his gaze reached Isabelle, who was standing at the far end of the room.

At that exact moment, as if sensing his presence, the bride-to-be glanced over, and the look they exchanged was electric, a fact that Angelica apparently wasn't alone in noticing; as the moment spun out, the conversation in the room slowly died off.

For endless seconds, the room remained hushed, and then Isabelle finally seemed to remember where—and who—she was. Lifting her chin, she looked away from Link and coolly addressed the group of women with whom she'd been conversing. "Pardon me a moment, won't you?" she said pleasantly. "I need to take care of this." Without waiting for a response, she turned and started toward the visitor.

As if released from a spell by her calm, deliberate manner, the hum of conversation once again began to rise, thankfully reaching normal levels by the time she reached the entry. Yet through some fluke of acoustics, Angelica could still clearly hear the conversation between Link and Isabelle.

"Hello Link." Despite her outward composure, Riley's sister's voice sounded slightly breathless.

"Isabelle." The investigator seemed to drink in the sight of her. "What are you doing here?"

"Some investigator you are," she said lightly, her mouth curving in a way that made her look remarkably like Riley. "Didn't you notice all the cars outside? Cynthia's throwing me a wedding shower."

"Ah. How nice for you." Although Templeton's voice was perfectly pleasant, there was something about the way he said it that suggested he wasn't completely sincere.

Isabelle clearly heard it, too. She lifted her chin slightly. "Yes, isn't it?"

Again they stared at each other, and the air around

them almost seemed to glitter with shooting sparks. "I should be going," Link said abruptly. "I was hoping to talk to Cynthia—" for the first time he glanced back into the room, belatedly registered Kate's and Angelica's presence and gave a nod of recognition "—but I can see this isn't a good time." He brought his gaze back to the slim young woman in the doorway. "Tell her I stopped by and that I'll call her later, will you?"

"Certainly."

"It's good to see you, Isabelle."

"Yes. You, too."

He turned on his heel and walked away. Isabelle watched him for a moment, then shut the door. When she turned, a spot of color stood high in both of her cheeks.

"Goodness," Kate murmured. "Is it my imagination, or is there a bit of chemistry between those two?"

"Maybe a little," Angelica said, feeling oddly protective of the younger woman. Telling herself it was because Isabelle was now her sister-in-law—and not because of her own recent, unsettling encounters with a certain good-looking man—she said firmly, "I'm sure it doesn't mean anything."

Kate glanced sharply at her. "Really? Why do you think that?"

She shrugged dismissively. "It's just that chemistry isn't everything. And Isabelle *is* marrying someone else."

Kate was silent, then gave a small sigh. "You know, my dear, by nature I'm a pragmatist. That's why it's taken me most of my life to learn that sometimes it's important to ignore your head and listen to what your heart is saying, instead. Unfortunately, it appears there's an excellent chance my darling Isabelle has yet to figure that out. Don't you make the same mistake.''

Angelica frowned, not quite sure how she'd become the object of Kate's concern. ''Pardon me?''

Kate reached for her punch and took a sip before she spoke. ''I'm very fond of your husband. The boy's a bit of a rogue, and not easy to know, but worth the effort, I think. I understand from Joan that the two of you didn't marry for conventional reasons, but I hope you'll give your marriage a chance. Pride doesn't keep you warm at night. Believe me, child, I know.''

The words struck too close to home. Angelica felt a pinch of dismay, even as she told herself not to be silly. There was no way Kate could know that she wasn't sleeping with Riley; the other woman had to be speaking metaphorically. And her words really didn't apply to Angelica's situation, anyway. Her reason for keeping Riley at a distance didn't have a thing to do with pride. It was a matter of self-preservation, pure and simple.

Wasn't it?

''And now that I've given you something to think about,'' Kate announced, climbing to her feet, ''I suppose I should mingle.'' Her eyes twinkled. ''It's expected of me, you know.''

''Well then, I wouldn't want to keep you.''

They smiled at each other and Kate reached over

to give her hand a squeeze. "You'll do, Angelica. Give that handsome husband a kiss for me, won't you?" She stood and walked away.

Bemused, Angelica stayed where she was, Kate's parting words lodged in her mind. She had a sudden vision of Saturday night, when she'd stood locked in Riley arms, her hands twined in his silky hair, her mouth glued to his...

Warmth spread through her and she abruptly asked herself what she was doing. It was bad enough that Riley seemed intent on driving her crazy; no way was she going to do it to herself.

Yet as she stood and went to find Cynthia to say her goodbyes, she knew it wasn't that simple. Because lately she'd begun to wonder if it was really Riley she was determined to keep at arm's length.

Or if, perhaps, it was her growing feelings for him.

Eight

———

The soft ripple of Angelica's laughter drifted down the hallway.

Riley paused as he stepped through the front door, his hand tightening on Cosmo's leash at the seductive sound.

He gave his head a slight shake—man, he was in sorry shape when something as run-of-the-mill as a simple giggle could make his pulse pick up—and looked down at the dog. "I suppose we should go say hello, huh?"

Cosmo grinned up at him, tail whipping in anticipation.

Riley wished he could match the dog's enthusiasm. But then he'd had better days.

A muscle jumped in his jaw as he thought again

about the meeting he'd had with Cynthia after work today. Although she was doing her best to remain optimistic, he knew damn well things weren't looking good for him legally. The case against him, though entirely circumstantial, was starting to seem overwhelming even to him—and he *knew* he was innocent. He didn't want to think about what was going to happen if the thing actually went to trial.

Rocking impatiently back on his heels, he ran a hand through his hair, hating his sense of powerlessness. There was no denying that something fraudulent had gone on for months on the Children's Hospital construction site, something that had cost Fortune Construction a bundle, something he should have caught. And no matter how often he reminded himself that it wasn't his job to scrutinize invoices or keep track of supplies, that the company paid several people good money to do just that, he couldn't help but think that if he'd just worked harder, paid more attention, been more vigilant, none of this— the fraud, Mike's death, his own current situation— would have happened. As it was, somebody had found it incredibly easy to frame him.

Which, he thought bleakly, they couldn't have done without help. Someone on the inside had to have been in on whatever had gone on. And since it wasn't him...

He blew out a frustrated breath, not liking the suspicion he'd entertained about Mike for a while now. And yet, unless Angelica's brother just happened to have been in the wrong place at the wrong time, he had to have died for *some* reason.

The one saving grace was that Angelica didn't seem to realize it. Nor did he intend to enlighten her. She'd been hurt enough by her brother's death. He hated to think how she'd react if his hunch about Mike turned out to be correct.

Cosmo jerked impatiently on the leash, snapping him out of his reverie. "What's the matter, buddy? You want to go join the action?" The dog tugged again and he sighed. "Okay, okay." He reached down, unclipped the lead and Cosmo promptly bounded away down the hall.

"Fickle dog," Riley muttered, following more slowly.

It was a sentiment that gained ground when he entered the family room and saw Cosmo happily greeting Chris Rogers.

With the boneless grace of youth, the kid was seated cross-legged at Angelica's feet on the floor by the coffee table, his back to the leather couch. Deepening Riley's disgust, the youngster gave a good-natured laugh as Cosmo took a swipe at his face with his pink doggy tongue.

"I'm glad to see you, too," Chris said, shoving the dog away.

That made one of them.

Angelica twisted around from her perch on the edge of the couch. "You're back."

"Yeah." Was it just wishful thinking, or did her eyes seem to brighten a little when she looked at him?

"How was your walk?"

"Okay. It's hot out there, though. I practically had to carry Cos the last mile home."

"Really?" Angelica's skeptical gaze skated over him. "You don't look like you did more than stroll around the block."

Damned if the dog didn't look over at him and appear to smile.

"In the first place, we live at the end of a cul-de-sac. In the second—" he glanced down at himself, pleased to see his loafers were dust free and the sleeves on his immaculate white shirt were still neatly rolled back "—Fortunes don't sweat. At least not from something as plebeian as dog-walking," he added, sending her an intimate look.

To his satisfaction, two little spots of color bloomed on her cheeks. Feeling more cheerful, he glanced past her at Rogers and forced himself to look friendly. "Hey, Chris. How you doing?"

"I'm okay."

"That your Jeep in the driveway?"

"Yeah. I bought it from my brother. It's a little beat, but I'm planning to fix it up."

"Yeah? Well, good for you. The first vehicle I ever owned was a Wrangler."

"*You* had a Jeep?"

"Yeah. Sure did. Had a hell of a good time with it, too." Right up until he'd rolled it one night taking a curve in Arroyo Canyon too fast. After that, he'd graduated to sports cars designed to take corners at a hundred-plus miles per hour.

The boy nodded with reluctant approval. "Cool."

"Yeah." He leaned down to pick a mud-colored

hair off his beige linen slacks and walked around to the sink to wash his hands. "Are you two getting hungry?"

"You bet," Chris said promptly at the same time Angelica said, "Maybe a little."

"Spaghetti sound all right?"

"You don't have to cook," Angelica protested. "We can order a pizza."

"I don't mind. Unless you'd prefer pizza."

"Spaghetti would be great," Chris offered.

To Riley's surprise, she shot the boy an irritated gaze. "Give him a break. He's worked all day," she informed him.

The kid flushed and sent Riley an apologetic look. "Sorry."

"Don't worry about it. I'm happy to do it. You two just go ahead and study. It shouldn't take me long to put things together."

Angelica worried her lower lip. "Are you sure?"

"Yeah. Just ignore me."

With a flattering air of reluctance, she slowly turned around and went back to work.

Something had changed in the handful of days since Isabelle's wedding shower, Riley thought as he put the sauce together, set it to simmer and began browning hamburger and onions. Although Angelica hadn't gone so far as to invite him to bed, she did seem to have lowered her guard. She was more open, more relaxed, less standoffish. Even more encouraging, he'd looked up more than once lately to find her watching him, a rapt expression on her face.

It might not be world peace—or an invitation to make love—but it would do for now.

He dumped the meat and onions into a colander to drain off the grease, then added it to the mixture. After checking the heat on the burner, he replaced the lid on the saucepan and walked over to open the refrigerator.

"It smells wonderful."

He glanced up as Angelica walked up beside him. "Thanks."

"Can I do anything to help?" She studied the fridge's interior.

He looked over his shoulder at the empty family room. "Where's your friend?"

"He went to take a quick swim. That's all right, isn't it?"

"Sure." He opened the crisper and began gathering the makings for a salad.

"You'll be happy to know—" she sent him a shrewd look "—that you improved your stock considerably with your car talk."

He shrugged. "Just a little male bonding." Turning, he gave the refrigerator door a nudge with his shoulder, managing to rub his thigh against hers in the process. "Sorry," he murmured insincerely.

She stepped back, but not before he heard her breath catch. "No problem."

He carried his cache of produce to the counter and got out the big glass salad bowl.

"I really would like to help," Angelica said, trailing after him.

"You can butter the French bread if you want."

"Great." As he began slicing vegetables, she got the bread from the drawer, then mixed together garlic, parsley, parmesan and margarine and spread it on the slices. "Can you hand me the foil?" she asked after they'd worked several minutes in companionable silence.

"No problem." He got the item out of the drawer and handed it to her, managing to graze her wrist with his fingers during the transfer. Her gaze flew briefly to his and lingered a moment before she looked away.

Realizing he'd forgotten to heat water for the noodles, he got a tall pot out of the cupboard. He filled it up, added a dollop of olive oil to keep it from boiling over and turned toward the cooktop at the same time that Angelica stepped back from sliding the bread into the oven. On the verge of bumping her with the heavy pot, he instinctively jerked back.

Water sloshed down his front. "Damn!" He hastily set down the pot.

"Oh, Riley!" Lips pursed in dismay, Angelica snatched up a kitchen towel, stepped close and began blotting at his chest. "You really nailed yourself."

"It's all right," he said, "it's just water."

"Yes, but you've been so great about everything. It doesn't seem fair." She patted a line from the vee of his shirt downward, her movements getting slower and slower the lower she went.

"Things could get a whole lot worse—or better, depending on your outlook—if you don't stop doing that," he said huskily.

Her hand stilled above his narrow gold belt buckle and she raised her gaze to his. Awareness and something else—uncertainty, apprehension, anticipation?—looked back at him from her soft green eyes. Her cheeks flushed; the pulse at the base of her throat began to speed up.

It was too good a chance to pass up. He leaned forward. Careful not to touch her anywhere else, determined not to scare her off, he angled his head and settled his mouth over hers.

He heard her inhale, but she didn't back away. Instead, after only the slightest hesitation, she began to kiss him back, her lips parting eagerly for his. A moment later, she brought her hand up and threaded her fingers into his hair, trailing her thumb over his cheek. A second after that her other hand stole around his neck.

With a light hand to the small of her back to keep her with him, he settled his back against the countertop, cradling her between his thighs.

He kissed her again, and it was sweet torment as her tongue met his and she took a step closer. Lost in each other, it was several long, delicious minutes before they surfaced for air.

Angelica leaned weakly against him. "Oh, my."

"Yeah." He felt a little light in the knees himself. But that didn't stop him from lowering his head and stringing a necklace of kisses along the fine-boned curve of her jaw.

"Riley, we shouldn't," she protested, even as her head fell back to allow him better access. "Not with Chris here."

He flicked his tongue against the shell of her ear. "I don't see him at the moment."

As if on cue came the sound of a woof. Glancing over, he saw Cosmo come trotting up to the slider with a wet Chris, towel slung around his neck, not far behind.

"Terrific," he muttered, turning back to Angelica. "How soon after dinner do you think we can get rid of him?"

She glanced at the window and back, and shook her head. "I'm afraid it doesn't matter. I have to be at work in an hour."

He sighed and tried not to look as frustrated as he felt. "I guess that means I'd better quit messing around, go change clothes and get the noddles on, huh?"

"I'm afraid so."

He nodded. Then, not giving her a chance to escape, he leaned down and kissed her again, this time hot and hard, making sure she wouldn't forget what she was missing.

When he finally set her away from him, she was breathing hard. "Later," he promised before setting off to change his shirt.

Feeling better than he had for days, he decided that if he could just stay out of prison, things might turn out okay.

Nine

The distinctive whine of the automatic garage door opener switching on filled the quiet house. Seated at the kitchen counter, textbooks spread out around her, Angelica went still as she heard it, then glanced at the oven clock.

She frowned. It was barely after three. In her admittedly limited experience, Riley normally didn't get home from work until at least five-thirty.

Anticipation filled her, nevertheless. Thanks to a late spring virus making the rounds, the Corral was currently short-handed, so she'd wound up working the dinner shift every night this week. She and Riley had barely seen each other since Monday night when he'd fixed spaghetti dinner.

Not that she'd missed him or anything, she was quick to assure herself.

Still, it would be nice to have a chance to talk, to hear about his week, to let him flirt with her. Plus there were several things she wanted to tell him.

She heard the door into the house open, then the sound of approaching footsteps. Marking her place in the child psych text she'd been studying, she tugged at the hem of her rose-colored tank dress, fleetingly wishing she was wearing something a little more substantial.

In the next instant, Riley walked into the room. She twisted around on the stool. "Hi," she said. "You're home early."

He dropped his sport coat over the back of the couch and tossed his keys on the counter. "Yeah, I am."

"How was your day?"

"I've had better." His voice clipped, his movements uncharacteristically stiff, he walked around the end of the counter, opened the fridge and grabbed a long-necked beer. He started to shut the door, then seemed to think better of it, reached in and grabbed a second bottle. "I'm going to go get out of these clothes." Without another word, he headed for the hall that led to the bedrooms.

Angelica sat frozen in place, wondering if she'd done something to offend him. Then she caught herself. The world didn't revolve around her, for one thing. More importantly, Riley had seemed perfectly fine this morning. Most likely he'd just had a bad day.

A really bad day.

The best thing she could do was give him some space.

She turned back around and opened her book. Finding her place, she again started to read yet another discussion regarding nature vs. nurture.

Her good intentions lasted a full nineteen minutes, when she realized she was listening for Riley's return rather than concentrating on the theories laid out before her. With a sigh, she pushed the book away. He'd had plenty of time to change. Where was he?

Telling herself it couldn't hurt to check on him, she climbed off the stool. She'd just ask what he'd like for dinner, make sure he was all right, then leave him alone.

Standing in the hallway a moment later, she found his bedroom door was ajar. She knocked softly.

There was no response. She hesitated, then knocked again, louder. This time when there was no answer, she pushed the door open and looked in.

The room appeared empty. She glanced toward the bathroom, but the door was open and there was no sign of movement. And then she saw the sheer draperies to the terrace flutter and realized that the French doors were open.

Her bare feet made no sound on the thick carpeting as she crossed the room and pushed the sheers aside. "Riley?" she said softly.

"What?"

He was sprawled on his back on the chaise longue on his private patio, one tanned arm covering his eyes. He'd changed, if you could call it that. She tried—and failed—not to stare at the sight of him wearing nothing but a pair of white shorts.

Her memory hadn't exaggerated his perfection. Contrasted with the shorts, his taut, unblemished skin was a beautiful bronzed gold color. He was wide at the shoulders and narrow at the hips, with the sort of washboard stomach usually only seen in body-building commercials. His hands and feet were long and tapering. And she knew for a fact that the parts of him she couldn't see were just as perfect.

It was suddenly hard to breathe.

"Aren't you due at work?" he inquired less than politely.

She dragged her gaze away from his torso, saying a prayer of thanks that his eyes were still covered. "I was, but..." She trailed off, not at all sure this was the time to share her news.

"But what?"

"I decided to take you up on your earlier offer, and take some time off. I told my boss last night."

He laughed mirthlessly. "Great."

She studied him. Lines she hadn't seen before were etched around his nose and mouth. "Riley, what's the matter?"

"Just let it go, Angelica, all right?"

"No. Is it your legal case? Has something happened?"

"Nope." For the first time his guard slipped and she heard a trace of bitterness in his voice. "I'm still the prime suspect."

"Then what's going on?"

He sighed, but lowered his arm. His gray gaze locked on her face. "You really want to know?"

"Yes."

"All right." He scooted up a little higher, reached for his beer and took a long pull before setting the bottle back on the accessory table at his elbow. "You're not the only one on hiatus from work. Count me in, too."

"*What?* Your cousins fired you?"

"No. Tyler and Jason would never do that. But…all the talk and speculation about what happened to Mike, and my alleged part in it, is a major distraction. At this point, my involvement in the firm makes it hard to get things done. And there are some serious discrepancies between the order logs and the on-site job invoices that need to be looked into—by somebody neutral, somebody who's not me. We had a meeting to talk about it and eventually we agreed that it would be best for the business if I took an extended vacation until this whole thing is…decided."

"Oh." It was clear he'd done what he thought was best for Fortune Construction. It was also very clear that, voluntary or not, the decision cut deep.

He must've seen the sympathy in her eyes because his own suddenly grew shuttered. "Not that it's a big deal. It's just a job. I'll survive."

She tried to think of something reassuring to say, but everything she came up with seemed trite. Nor did it help that there was a part of her that felt off-balance and distracted, thanks to the display of masculine perfection laid out before her.

Suddenly realizing she was staring at his navel, which was an absolutely a perfect oval anchored by a thin arrow of black hair that disappeared suggestively under his waistband, she forced herself to look away and found him watching her.

Ashamed—he finally opened up, and she was too busy lusting after his body to think of the right thing to say—she looked guiltily away.

"Relax," he said sarcastically, misreading her reaction. "I'm not going to jump you. I've had my share of being shot down today." His mouth twisted and he reached for his beer again.

And just like that, she couldn't stand it. She instinctively reached out and grabbed his wrist. "Don't."

He looked at her, a study in arrested motion. "Don't what? Don't be so pathetic? Or don't get drunk?" He didn't wait for an answer. "Sorry, babe, but there's nothing I can do about the first, and as for the other—" he shrugged dismissively "—I've got a reputation to maintain."

She tightened her grip on his wrist. "You're not pathetic," she said firmly. "And as for getting drunk... There are better ways to cope with this."

His eyes narrowed. "Like what?"

"We could...talk."

"Oh, yeah. That'll help." Their gazes locked; he glanced deliberately at her mouth, then back into her eyes. "Don't toy with me, Angelica. Not today."

She swallowed. "I'm not."

"Yeah, right."

Maybe it was the grim note in his voice. Or

maybe it was the bleak look that flashed across his face, but she knew she had to do something. Not giving herself time to think, she leaned over, braced her hand against the chaise cushion to one side of his head, closed her eyes and pressed her mouth to his.

Time seemed to stop. She felt the warm breeze tickle over her bare legs and arms, heard the pool filter switch on, felt Riley stiffen with shock. Then his hand came up to grip the back of her head, holding her against him as his mouth slanted hungrily against hers in a drugging kiss.

Heat spiraled through her, leaving her as boneless as warmed butter. Her arm buckled, bringing her to rest against the hard curve of his chest. Confronted with all that bare skin, she couldn't resist touching him. Her palm skated slowly from his armpit to the rounded bulge of his shoulder. His skin felt like heated velvet, and she exhaled with pleasure.

He made a sound low in his throat and half-tugged, half-lifted her on top of him. She gasped as she found herself straddling him, her dress rucked up around her waist, his muscular midriff sliding hot and hard and evocative against her bare thighs.

With a clarity that was as surprising as everything else that was happening, she knew there wouldn't be any pulling back. And not because Riley would likely never forgive her if she did. But because *she* didn't want to stop.

The realization jolted through her. For a moment she felt overcome with panic, and then it faded away. She still might not understand why he'd taken off the way he had that night three months ago, but she knew that it wasn't because he was just some selfish playboy who'd been out to score.

What's more, though she knew he'd be the first to deny it, he cared deeply about a number of things. His home, his family, his job, their baby. He might not be the hero she'd made him out to be as a teen, but he wasn't her enemy, either. He was her husband, and—she caught her breath—she cared about him.

What's more, Kate had been right; pride *didn't* keep you warm at night. She'd missed this. She'd missed *him,* and she couldn't pretend otherwise any longer.

"Angel. *Angel.*" His mouth clung to hers as if he were drowning and she was his only hope for rescue.

She kissed him back, parting her lips for his tongue. She could taste the beer he'd been drinking, and something that was uniquely Riley. The latter made her feel light-headed and she kissed him over and over again, drinking in the heat of his mouth, reveling in their mutual hunger. She couldn't seem to get enough.

His hand came up and found her breast. She shivered with delight as he rubbed the pad of his thumb over the thin layers of cotton and nylon covering her nipple. Catching the sensitive peak between his fingers, he gently squeezed.

Her body rioted. She bit back a moan, pressing against him as she felt a throbbing ache bloom between her thighs. "Riley, don't," she said breathlessly.

His hand stilled instantly. "What's wrong?" he said raggedly, breathing hard. "I didn't hurt you, did I?"

"No, of course not. It's just…too much."

His expression changed, going from concern to satisfied in an instant. "Ah. Well we wouldn't want that." To her surprise, he pushed her into a sitting position. Grabbing the hem of her dress, he pulled it up over her head and tossed it away, the skin across his nose tightening as he looked at her. "Damn, but you're beautiful."

He reached around and unsnapped her bra with one practiced movement. Tugging the lacy garment away, he cupped her breasts in his hands, pushed them together, and pressed his mouth to the valley he'd created. Then, before she could divine his intent, he lowered his head, took one nipple into his mouth and suckled.

The sensation produced by his mouth was ten times more intense than that from his hand. The steady rhythm made her tremble. Unable to stay still, she rocked against him, flushing a little as she felt the slick dampness between her thighs—and the hard ridge of his sex beneath her. Her mouth went dry with need.

As if he could read her mind, he lifted his head. "I want you, Angel."

"Yes."

"I want you *now,* but you have to want me back." His gaze was fierce, his voice a low rasp.

"Yes. Oh, yes, Riley, I do," she assured him fervently.

Without further delay he lifted his hips, shoved down his shorts and underwear and kicked them away.

The heat rising off his skin was shocking. So was the way he reached down, snapped the thin nylon ties on the sides of her panties and yanked them away.

She felt him, hot and insistent, and then he was lifting her, bracing himself, and guiding her down.

Clutching his shoulders, she slid onto the thickness of him. She bit her lip, her eyes fluttering shut at the fullness of his slow, measured invasion as she felt her body stretch to accommodate him.

She felt the wildness start to burn through her blood, a swift rush of passion that in all her life only he'd been able to tap. But threaded through it was tenderness, a need to give, to share herself with this one special man. Leaning down, she caught his lip between her teeth and came up on her knees.

His body bucked, but she refused to be rushed, determined to draw the moment out. She took him slowly, savoring every velvety, rock-hard inch until finally he was sheathed to the hilt.

His control snapped. Grabbing her hips, he urged her up, then pressed her down, his back arching as he rose to meet her. Then he did it again and her every thought of taking things slow vanished, replaced by the white-hot need for him that had ignited inside her.

"Damn." His head fell back and his body bowed. "Angelica. Baby. Don't stop."

She looked down. His eyes were shut, his inky

hair was plastered to his damp forehead and his mouth was wet from their kisses. Something inside her seemed to give way like a wall coming down, and emotion flooded her, hot and tender, and then she was crying out. Pleasure caught her, tightly budded at first, then uncurling, expanding, rocketing outward.

Riley's arms came around her. His hips slammed up and she heard him cry out. Then his mouth found hers and, holding tight, they rode out the wave together.

It had been a hell of a day, Riley thought, as he lay sprawled on his bed with Angelica's warm, boneless body cradled against him.

He didn't remember exactly when they'd moved inside. Or how. Except for the sheet twisted over their hips, the rest of the covers had wound up on the floor, along with the bedspread and all but the single pillow they shared. The past few hours were blurred in his mind, a collage of passion given and pleasure taken.

Yawning, he considered the moonlight pouring into the room and the warm, desert breeze whispering in through the open French doors, and realized he must have slept. But then, that wasn't surprising. His wife had worn him out.

A faint, satisfied smile curved his mouth. Having sex with Angelica had been every bit as good as he'd remembered. It had been hot and fast, wet and wild, slow and generous; in every way she'd proven his perfect match.

And though that might have bothered him as recently as a week ago, tonight he was finally all right with it. After all, he'd been thinking of little else for the past two weeks, so his satisfaction was only natural. Once the newness had worn off, he imagined some of the current, extraordinary magic between them would dissipate as well.

As for the other feelings coursing through his blood—the strong sense of possessiveness, the tenderness, the powerful need he had to be with her and nobody else—he was all right with that, too, for now.

Because now that he could think again, he realized that things were different than they had been three and a half months ago. Angelica was going to be the mother of his child, after all. It made sense that he'd want to protect her, take care of her, be with her. The fact that he also felt better than he had for a long, long time was just icing on the cake.

He felt Angelica stir. "You awake?" he asked softly.

"Mm-hmm."

He shifted, rolling onto his side and settling her back against his front, bringing his hand to rest on her stomach.

She gave a happy sigh and snuggled against him. "This is nice."

"What?"

"Just lying here together like this."

"Yeah."

She placed her hand over his. "Another month and you should be able to feel the baby moving."

"Really?" Up until now, when he'd thought about having a kid it had been mostly in the abstract, as a responsibility to undertake, an obligation to protect. Now, all of a sudden, he pictured a little girl with Angelica's green eyes and his own dark hair, and it made his throat go tight. "You don't think we hurt anything, going at it like that, do you?"

"No, of course not." She paused. "Besides, I saw my doctor the day before we got married, and he said making love was all right."

"You asked him?"

"Of course not." She tried to sound offended, but he could hear the smile in her voice. "He volunteered it."

His own mouth quirked. "Well, that's good."

"Mm-hmm." She stretched. "Riley?"

"Hmm?"

"I'm sorry about your job."

"Yeah, I know." He stroked his hand over a strand of her long hair; the shiny strands clung to his fingers. "But it didn't turn out all bad. If I'd known pity would get you back into bed with me, I'd have gotten myself cut loose a whole lot sooner."

"Riley!" she protested with a laugh.

He chuckled in turn and tightened his arms around her. After a moment, he admitted thoughtfully, "The thing is...I don't know what I'm going to do with all my spare time. If you didn't have finals and I wasn't out on bail—" try as he might, he couldn't keep a sardonic note out of his voice

"—we could go on a honeymoon. As it is, we're stuck."

She gave his hand a squeeze. "It doesn't matter to me. Your house is nicer than most resorts. And no matter where we are, we can use some time to get better acquainted. Besides, as perfect as it seems to me, there must be something you want to get done around here."

"Yeah, I suppose. I should figure out how to safeguard the pool, which will make my mother happy. And I could get started on the baby's room, maybe paint it or something."

"See, there you go. It'll be all right. You'll see." They were both quiet for a moment, and then Angelica spoke again. "Riley?"

"Hmm?"

"The first time we were together…why did you just take off like that? And why didn't you call me later?"

Somehow he'd expected the question. But that didn't mean he had to like it. "I don't know. There were lots of reasons. I guess I just felt…you'd been through enough. You didn't need someone like me complicating your life."

"Oh." Clutching the sheet, she rolled over onto her stomach and propped herself up on her elbow to look at him. "So you did it for my own good?"

He had the grace to wince. "No—yes—hell, I don't know, Angelica. I didn't do it to hurt you." That, at least, was the truth. "The important thing is, it's over. In the past. Can't we just forget about it? At least for tonight?"

She searched his face, and after a moment, she nodded. "All right."

He breathed a sigh of relief. "Good. Because I can think of a lot of better things to do than rehash the past."

"You can?" She didn't look convinced.

"Yeah."

"Like what?"

"Ever gone swimming naked under the stars?"

"No."

"Never?"

She shook her head. "Never."

He tossed the sheet away, climbed out of the bed and reached for her hand. "Well, lady—that's about to change."

Ten

"**O**h, look!" Angelica clutched Riley's thigh as the Ferris wheel stopped to allow more passengers to board, leaving their gently swaying wooden seat poised at the top of the ride's arc. "You can see the lights from downtown. Isn't it pretty?"

Riley looked at her indulgently. "Yeah, I guess. Although if you're really impressed by the lights of Pueblo, I think you need to get out more."

"Thanks a lot," she said, settling back in the drape of his arm with a good-natured laugh.

The wicked grin that always made her heart beat faster flashed across his face, showing off the grooves in his cheeks that he'd firmly informed her were *not* dimples. "You're welcome."

She felt her own face soften as she looked at him,

and she was very much afraid that her heart was in her eyes. She forced herself to look away, but even as her gaze focused on the spectacle around them— the brilliant array of twirling, spinning, colored lights from the other rides on the midway, the crowd strolling along down below while brightly dressed barkers vied loudly for their attention—her thoughts stayed with him and the past week.

It had been the most wonderful five days of her life. Among other things, though she'd still had studying to do, they'd also gone to a movie, made love, played in the pool, made love, shopped for the baby's room, made love, talked, made love, given Cosmo a bath—and made love.

Actually, when she stopped to think about it, as absorbed as they'd been with each other—and as inventive and tireless as her husband was—it was remarkable they'd ever gotten out of bed.

"What are you smiling about?" Riley inquired.

For half a second, she almost told him. But then her better sense kicked in. When it came to sex, the last thing Riley needed was to have his ego stroked; he knew very well how good he was. "Just all of this." She indicated the carnival spread out below them with a wave of her hand. "It makes me feel as if I'm sixteen again."

"Was that the last time you went to a carnival?"

"That's the *only* time I went to a carnival."

"You're kidding."

"No. And as it was, getting to go at all was just a matter of luck. Not only did my dad happen to be sober at the right time, but he was actually working, which didn't happen very often, and he decided to treat Mike and me. It was really fun. Of course,'' she added with a philosophical shrug, ''the very next day he started drinking again, and by the time the carnival came to town two years later he and my mom had had their car accident and they were both gone.''

His arm tightened around her ever so slightly. ''I'm sorry, Angel.''

''Don't be. It's been long enough that it doesn't hurt anymore. And I'll always have that one great memory. With my family, I learned early to count my blessings, no matter how small.'' The Ferris wheel gave a jerk, setting their seat rocking as it descended several feet before again stopping. ''What about you?'' she asked. ''Were you a carnival-goer? Or are Fortunes too sophisticated for that?''

''Oh, I came all right, every year until I was fifteen. Girls like carnivals and I liked girls. Still do.''

''What happened when you were fifteen?''

''I got in trouble and got booted out. As usual.''

She considered his matter-of-fact expression. ''Let me guess. Did you try to sneak in? Or cheat at one of the games? Or try to take a second turn on a ride without paying?'' Among the kids in the neighborhood she'd grown up in, all of those things had been standard fare.

''Give me some credit,'' he said with mock indignation. ''I got away with all that. What I got caught at was being behind the bleachers with Marianne Milkowski with my pants down—literally.

Unfortunately, the head of security was her uncle, so I was persona non grata after that.''

''Oh dear.'' She did her best to look solemn, but couldn't entirely hide a smile.

As the Ferris wheel finally began to move without interruption, he took note of her amusement and did his best to look offended, but the effect was ruined as his arm tightened around her, pulling her even closer. ''Hey, laugh if you want to, but my folks didn't think it was so funny. They were furious. I can still remember the lecture my dad gave me about my lack of responsibility. Which wasn't nearly as bad as when my mom told me how disappointed she was.''

She had yet to meet his father, but from just two meetings she knew that his mother adored him. ''I'm sure they weren't as upset with you as you thought. They were probably just trying to make an impression.''

''I don't think so. They never got that kind of grief from Shane. But no matter how hard I tried, I just couldn't seem to stay out of trouble.'' Although his voice was still light, there was an undercurrent there that caught her by surprise. To her shock, she realized that he wasn't nearly as nonchalant about his childhood transgressions as he wanted her to think.

''Don't be so hard on yourself. From what you've told me, it wasn't as if you were in a gang or committed arson or robbed a convenience store. Besides, it was a long time ago, and now you're a responsible, hard-working adult.''

"Oh, yeah. Except for the fact that I happen to be out on bond for murder, I'm a real paragon." The undercurrent was stronger now, just a hint of self-directed distaste that made her hurt for him.

"I'm sure the truth will come out," she said, praying it was true and feeling a pang of guilt as she thought about the remainder of Mike's things that she had yet to go through.

"Maybe." He gave a shrug that sent their seat rocking. "But the one thing I know—" he managed a good imitation of his usual devil-may-care smile "—is that I'm not going to let it ruin our evening. Okay?"

She studied his face, then nodded, seeing how genuinely it mattered to him. "Okay."

"So what do you want to do next?"

"I don't know. Maybe get some cotton candy?"

"You're kidding, right?"

"No."

"Maybe it's slipped your mind, but you've already had a snow cone, a caramel apple and a giant pretzel, and that was just in the last hour."

"Don't be a spoilsport," she said sweetly. "In case you've forgotten, I'm eating for two. Not to mention that I need my strength to keep up with you."

"Poor baby. Have I been wearing you out the past few days?"

The concern in his eyes made her feel warm all over. So did the way he gathered her closer, so that her head rested against the curve of his shoulder. With a sense of wonder, she realized she'd never felt more secure in her life. "I think I'll survive," she said softly.

He traced a circle on her arm with his fingertip. "You're not sorry, are you?"

"About what?"

"That we made love?"

"Which time?"

He sent her a chiding look. "Angel."

She smiled. "No. Not at all. But I'm not sorry we waited a few weeks, either.

"It felt a hell of a lot longer than that to me."

"That's because patience isn't your strong suit," she teased.

His elegant black eyebrows rose in reproof. "That's not what you said last night."

A burst of heat went through her at the reminder. They'd been out by the pool, watching the stars as they lay side-by-side on the deck. And then he'd kissed her, and one thing had led to another... "That was then and this is now," she said primly. "Although, if you're really nice to me, keep me fed and maybe win me one of those cute pink snakes I've seen people carrying around, you could get lucky tonight and have a chance to show me what you can do."

"I could, huh?"

The Ferris wheel began to slow. "Yes, I think so."

He tipped his head and kissed her. "One cotton candy and one snake coming up," he promised as he finally pulled away.

Angelica wasn't sure if it was a threat or a promise.

Then again, she didn't care. She was too busy looking forward to later.

Angelica gently rubbed her thumb over the snapshot of Mike's smiling face. She'd come across the photo of him, beaming in his cap and gown at his high school graduation, just seconds ago. It had been stuck in the middle of a pile of auto part receipts and it had caught her by surprise.

Unexpectedly, tears prickled her eyes. She blinked them back and told herself now was not the time to get sentimental. Even if it was perfectly understandable, given how tired she was. But then in the three days since the carnival, between finals—she'd taken her last one yesterday afternoon—and making love with Riley, she hadn't been getting a lot of sleep.

She could have slept in this morning, she supposed. But when Riley had told her last night that he had some errands to run today, and that as long as he was out he thought he'd drop by the athletic club and see if he could scare up a racquetball game, she'd known what she had to do.

With one last bittersweet glance, she added Mike's photo to the small pile of things she'd set aside to keep, and tossed the receipts back in the box she'd taken them from. Climbing to her feet, she carried the box over and set it with the rest of the containers to be discarded that were now stacked near the door. As she turned around and saw that there were only two boxes left to go through, a ker-nel of panic blossomed in the pit of her stomach.

With sudden clarity, she realized that while she may have told herself she wanted to know the truth, when she'd first started going through Mike's things there'd been a part of her that had hoped she wouldn't find anything. On some level she'd had her fingers crossed that her suspicions about her brother would prove groundless.

Then, in those first few days after she and Riley had gotten married, when she'd really started to hope she'd find something, it had been mostly for the baby, because she hadn't wanted her child to grow up thinking his or her father was a murderer.

But now, what she wanted most in the world was to give Riley his life back. If that meant exposing her brother as less than honest, if it meant proving once and for all that the Dodds really were nothing but trailer trash, she'd live with it.

Because she loved Riley, and nothing mattered more than that.

As she knelt and yanked the lid off the nearest box, she found herself praying fervently that she'd find something. She looked down, and a half-dressed, come-hither model on the cover of a glossy girlie magazine stared back at her, topping what looked to be a substantial pile of more of the same. More disappointed than disgusted, wondering what had ever possessed her to pack this lot, she started to replace the lid, then stopped.

It would be foolish to quit being thorough at this point. So with a sigh, she reached in and rifled through the stack. She wasn't really surprised, however, when, except for a trio of auto rebuild manuals and a single copy of *Investors Weekly*, all she found were more magazines boasting half-naked cover girls.

Discouraged, she let the magazines fall back into the box and pushed it away. Crossing her fingers that the best had been saved for last, she reached for the remaining box and pulled off the lid.

The result wasn't encouraging. Like most of the others that she'd been through, this one appeared to contain a jumble of odds and ends and what looked to be a ream of miscellaneous papers.

Knowing it was probably a waste of time, but not about to quit—there was still a chance, she told herself fiercely—she lifted out a messy heap of papers and began to separate them into piles. Finding yet another fistful of money order stubs, her brother's preferred way of paying his bills, she shook her head. Mike's finances had always teetered on the edge of disaster, not surprising when he'd lacked even enough self-discipline to handle a checking account.

So what on earth would he want with a copy of *Investors Weekly*?

The errant thought froze her in place for one endless second.

Then she leaned forward, grabbed the box of magazines and dragged it toward her. Rocking back on her heels, she reached in and sorted through the stack until she found the magazine in question. She pulled it out and started to fan through the pages.

It didn't take long for her to find what she was looking for. Inserted in the middle of the slick pages was a single sheet of lined notebook paper, folded in half. She pulled it out, her heart pounding as she saw that taped to the page beneath it was a flat silver skeleton key. A tag was attached. She turned it over and Mike's cramped handwriting leapt out at her. First Central Bank, Rio Hermosa Br., Tucson, 442. It had to refer to a safety deposit box, she realized.

For a moment she just sat there, stunned, excited, hopeful, yet also filled with dread at the possible implications of her discovery. Taking a deep breath, she set down the magazine with its unexpected key and picked up the piece of paper.

She opened it up with hands that shook and saw a neat list of dated entries. Most of them appeared to be a straightforward record of money received, totaling what at a glance looked to be more than twenty-five thousand dollars. Stunned by the dollar amount, it took her a moment to realize that here and there her brother had added an observation. With a sinking feeling, she slowly began to read through them.

Sept. 5—A grand and all it took was my signature and a little paper shuffling. Man, is this easy money or what?

Sept. 18—Signed off on another shipment. Piece of cake. I like it.

Oct. 21—Damned if I didn't almost get caught by Jason Fortune this morning. I talked my way out of it, but I've told the Boss it's gonna cost him. I deserve it.

Dec. 15—A double damn Christmas bonus. Bitchin'!

Jan. 5—Mr. Riley Fortune himself was here today, walking around, poking into things. He thinks he's so cool, but the jokes on him. The smug S.O.B. doesn't have a clue.

Jan. 18—Told the Boss $5000 a pop won't fly anymore. He's raking it in while I take all the chances. It's my butt on the line, and I let him know it.

Feb 2—Gave the Boss an ultimatum. Either he cuts me in big-time and gives me one million dollars or I go have a little talk with the good old VP of Finance and open his eyes to what's going on right under his Fortune nose.

Angelica squeezed her eyes shut. *Oh, Mike, how could you? For the first time in your life you had a decent job and a shot at a decent life, and you threw it all away for some fast money.*

Nevertheless, the implication was clear. Mike had been dead less than a week after that final entry. Not only had he clearly been in on some sort of scam to cheat the Fortunes, but when he'd tried to shake down the "Boss"—whoever that was—the man must have had enough and decided to put a permanent end to his problem.

Yet even in the midst of her shame at Mike's actions, and her sorrow at his needless death, she felt a growing sense of elation, since the entries also made it clear that Riley was innocent in all of this.

And though there was still a chance he might despise her when he learned that her brother had been swindling his company, and was therefore partly responsible for his current legal jeopardy, there was no question about what she had to do.

Climbing to her feet, she went to call Cynthia.

Eleven

"**So.**" Sinking down on the couch next to Angelica, Riley stretched out his legs and slung his arm behind her. "Are you going to tell me what's bothering you or not?"

He wasn't a bit surprised when she tensed. She'd been on pins and needles ever since he'd walked in the door an hour and a half ago. At first he'd thought she was mad at him because he'd played an extra game of racquetball and gotten home later than planned. But when he'd looped his arm around her neck and drawn her close for a kiss, she'd responded with such unbridled passion that he'd known that wasn't it.

Then things had gotten interesting and he'd forgotten to be concerned about anything but the sweetness of her mouth and the ardor of her response.

Until the doorbell rang and she'd stiffened up as if she were expecting a SWAT team to rush in and drag her away.

Perplexed, and more than a little annoyed by the interruption, he'd stalked to the door to find his mother and Isabelle had dropped by for a visit. And though Angelica had made an obvious effort to be a good hostess, the longer they'd stayed the quieter she'd become.

But now the female members of his family were finally gone and he intended to get some answers.

He watched as she dampened her lips with the tip of her tongue. "Why do you think something's bothering me?" she said carefully.

He slid his hand under the glossy cloak of her hair and gently kneaded her nape. "Because you're jumpier than a pogo stick."

She angled her head to look at him, a strained smile on her face. "Am I really that obvious?"

"I don't think my mom or Isabelle noticed, but yeah, you are to me."

Her expression seemed to turn inward once again. "I see."

He waited, but when she didn't immediately say anything more, his impatience got the better of him. "Is everything all right with the baby?"

She looked up, startled. "Yes, of course."

"Then whatever it is, it can't be that bad," he said flatly.

"It's not bad at all," she said in a rush. "Actually, it's good. Maybe even great."

"Then what?"

She knit her fingers together, let out a pent-up breath and turned toward him, her gaze locking on his face. "You know the boxes you moved out of the garage for me?"

"Yeah."

"They weren't mine and I wasn't looking for class notes. That is, they are mine, but the stuff in them is Mike's. Nothing very important, just miscellaneous things that were in various drawers or just sitting around his apartment that I should have gone through after he died. Except that I didn't. I just...couldn't at the time."

She paused, looking at him as if to make sure he understood, and he nodded, although he couldn't imagine where this was going.

She swallowed nervously. "The thing is...a few days before he died, Mike said something that really bothered me, about how he was going to come into some big money. He always believed he was smarter than everybody else, and when he said that, it made me think he was involved in something he shouldn't be. And then, after he died, even though the police went through his things eventually, I couldn't help but wonder if they'd missed something. I kept thinking it would be just like Mike to make some sort of record of what was going on, that it would increase his sense of outsmarting everyone." She shrugged unhappily. "I guess you just had to know him to understand."

Riley didn't know what to say. All this time she'd been carrying this around inside her and she'd never said a word? "That's why you've been going through the boxes?"

"Yes."

"Why didn't you tell me?"

Two dots of color flooded her pale cheeks, but her voice remained steady. "Because I wasn't sure about anything. And if nothing turned up, I didn't want to get your hopes up. And because—" her chin rose a fraction of an inch "—even though I'm not proud of it, part of me was hoping I wouldn't find anything. I just didn't want to believe that my brother had done something wrong." Her shoulders sagged. "But then, this morning, I found it."

"You found what?"

"Proof that Mike *was* involved in something. He left a record of the amounts of money he was getting from someone he called the Boss—and he wrote some things down that make it clear that the Boss isn't you, that you're weren't a part of what was going on. I also found the key to a safety deposit box in Tucson."

It took a good long moment for what she was saying to sink in. When it finally did, he suddenly found himself on his feet, adrenaline rushing through him. "Where is this stuff? I want to see it."

She shook her head. "I called Cynthia, who called Link, and they came and got it."

"What? Dammit, Angelica, you should have waited until I got home! You should've let me look at it."

"I couldn't! Cynthia thought this might be how you'd react and she didn't want you involved. She was afraid it might raise questions, further compromise an already questionable chain of evidence and come back on you somehow. She was adamant.''

He stared at her in disbelief, his mind racing in a dozen different directions. ''Even so—''

The phone rang and they both jumped. He gave her one long, searching look and then stalked across the floor and snatched up the phone, ready to take the caller's head off for the interruption. *''What?''*

''Riley?''

Cynthia's mellow voice had its usual grounding effect. He took a deep breath, got a hold on his emotions and forced himself to respond with a semblance of calm. ''Yeah, it's me.''

''Have you and Angelica had a chance to talk?'' she asked tactfully in her best lawyer's voice.

''Yeah.''

''Good. Because I just got off the phone with Link Templeton, who called me from Tucson, and I've got wonderful news.''

He didn't say anything, just waited.

''Link got a court order to open Mike's safety deposit box, and he says he's got the evidence to clear you. He's calling the D.A.'s office right now and recommending they drop all of the charges against you.''

The blood roared in his ears and he squeezed his eyes shut, so overcome that for a moment he was absolutely incapable of a response.

''Riley, are you there? Did you hear what I said?''

He sucked in a breath and struggled to get a handle on his cartwheeling emotions. ''Yeah, yeah, I did." He opened his eyes. "So who is it? Who was Dodd involved with? Is it somebody we know?"

"Link wouldn't say. He says that while it's clear that one of your main suppliers was overbilling the company, charging Fortune Construction for double or triple the amount of materials than were actually delivered, and that the scheme worked because Mike was getting paid to sign off on the shipments, he still has some details to nail down before he's willing to name the murderer. And that even once he knows for sure, any announcement ought to come through official channels, not him. Personally, I doubt he'll be able to keep the lid on this much longer, but he refused to budge."

"But you're sure I'm in the clear?"

Cynthia's businesslike tone softened. "Absolutely. I'm going to call the D.A. myself as soon as we hang up. It'll probably take a few days, but by next Monday we should be able to go back into court and have the charges officially withdrawn. By this time next week it ought to be all over."

"You're sure?" he repeated, still not quite daring to believe it.

"Yes. Link wouldn't have called me, and I wouldn't have called you, if I wasn't. It's over, Riley. This whole horrible nightmare is finally over."

He blew out a noisy breath. "Wow."

"Yeah." Cynthia's calm, above-the-fray lawyer facade slipped a little more and she was no longer able to contain her elation. "Wow is right. And now I have a favor to ask."

"Anything."

"Is it all right with you if I call and tell Shane? He's been so worried."

"Hell, Cynthia, of course. You can call Shane and Mom and Dad and anyone else you want to. And even though I know it's not enough—thank you. For everything."

"I'm so happy for you," she said warmly. "Take some time to celebrate, and I promise I'll call the instant I hear anything more."

"Thanks."

She disconnected and he hung up his own receiver. Turning slowly around, he found Angelica staring at him, her face taut with strain. "Is—is everything okay?"

He looked at her and relief began to give way to exhilaration. "Yeah. Cynthia says they're going to drop the charges." He heard himself say the words and suddenly couldn't contain a smile. "She says it's over."

"Oh, Riley!" As if released by his smile from an invisible bond, she dashed across the room and threw herself into his arms. "That's wonderful!"

The smile became a grin and he suddenly felt on top of the world. "Yeah, it is." He still had at least a dozen unanswered questions—and a small, nagging feeling of uneasiness that he was damned if he understood—but he was in no mood for introspection.

Lifting Angelica off her feet, he swung her around, making her laugh with delight. Looking down into her happy face, desire swept through him, hot and overwhelming.

He gave in to temptation without a second thought, leaned over and kissed her. She gave a little gurgle of surprised pleasure, and then her arms tightened around his neck and she was kissing him back.

Minutes later, generally feeling wonderful, he began to back toward the refrigerator.

Angelica raised her head. "What are you doing?"

"Celebrating." Setting her on her feet, he opened the fridge door and retrieved the bottle of champagne he'd bought for their aborted wedding night. He ripped off the foil and worked the cork free. There was a hollow pop and then the fizzy wine bubbled up, running over his hand and dripping onto the floor.

Angelica laughed. "Riley!"

"Want some?"

She shook her head. "I'm not drinking these days, remember?"

"Ah, that's right." He raised the bottle to his mouth and took a quick swig and the fuzzy wine exploded in his stomach, sending heat through his veins. Grabbing her hand, he began tugging her toward the couch. "Come on."

"What are we doing?"

He shoved the coffee table out of the way with his foot. "I'm going to give you a lesson on an alternate way to enjoy champagne."

"Oh? And what's that?"

"Take off your clothes and I'll show you."

She gave him a long look, part amusement, part excitement. "Only if you do, too."

"Not a problem." He set the champagne bottle

on the end table and yanked his shirt over his head. Naked in about nine seconds flat, he reached over and steadied Angelica as she stepped out of her panties and shorts.

"Thank you."

"My pleasure. Now lie down."

She gave him another look but did as he said, shivering a little as she came in contact with the smooth leather couch. "It's cold."

"Don't worry, I'll warm you up, I promise." Grabbing the champagne bottle, he knelt down beside her and poured a thimble's worth of wine into the well of her navel.

"Riley!"

"Hush, baby." He leaned over and sucked the bubbly liquid into his mouth, then poured another dollop and did it again, his hand skating up to cradle her breast.

"Oh, my," she said breathlessly.

"Not too bad, huh?" He tipped the bottle again, only this time he let it trickle lower than her navel before bowing his head and licking it from her skin.

"Oh!" Her hips suddenly bucked as he chased a bead of champagne downward. "Riley!" she cried again.

"Trust me. You'll like this," he said. He sure did. His heart was thumping like a jackhammer as he took his time, tasting her, finding her more intoxicating than any bottle of wine. But then, he felt more than a little drunk, with happiness and relief—not to mention the soft mewling sound she made as he settled his mouth over her and his tongue breached the seat of her desire.

Her hips bucked again, and she was suddenly tugging on his hair. "Now," she said with a fierce sob as he reluctantly looked up. "I want you inside me."

She didn't have to ask twice. He clambered onto the couch to settle between her thighs. Bracing his weight on his hands, he leaned down and kissed her as he slid inside her, both of them groaning as they came together. Wrapping her legs around his waist, she reached up and tried to pull him even closer, but it was impossible on the narrow confines of the couch.

Making a quick decision, he rolled them onto the floor, holding her tight and breaking her fall with his body. Then he shifted her beneath him, still inside her, reached for her hands and entwined his long fingers with her smaller ones.

She looked up at him, and there was a look on her face he'd never seen before. "I love you, Riley." She raised her head and pressed a kiss to his mouth, her lips clinging to his with a sort of aching tenderness that stole his breath. "No matter what happens, I love you so much."

The words took him by surprise. They seemed to detonate inside him, setting off a chain reaction of need. Not knowing what to say, he bowed his head and kissed her back, a flood of possessiveness sweeping through him. He began to move, his hips pumping, slowly at first, then faster and faster as he

tried to get closer, deeper, needing something...
needing her...

They rocked together, mouths sealed, hands
clasped, bodies growing slick from exertion as the
world seemed to fade away and there was just the
two of them, together.

And then Angelica cried out. Her arms tightened
around him, and she shuddered, and her explosion
set off his own. He pressed himself deeply inside
her, his head falling back as her body tightened
around him. Then his climax ripped through him,
pleasure so sweet it brought tears to his eyes and
had him clenching his teeth.

Contractions racked him, until at last all the
strength seemed to drain out of him and he collapsed
against her, still holding tight to her hands. He had
just enough presence of mind to roll onto his side,
and then for a space of time his mind went blank,
done in by the extent of his pleasure.

When he finally opened his eyes he found Angelica was watching him, the tenderness he'd felt
earlier in her kiss now reflected in her eyes. "You
were right." Her voice was raspy with exhausted
satisfaction. But that didn't stop her as she reached
out and gently stroked her fingers through his hair,
brushing it back from his temple.

"About what?"

She smiled. "There is more than one way to enjoy
champagne."

He couldn't help but smile back.

Riley glanced sideways at his wife. She lay facing
him, her head pillowed on her arm, fast asleep on

the thick pile of the family room carpet.

Careful not to disturb her, he shifted more fully onto his back and stared at the ceiling overhead.

Except for the gentle hum of the refrigerator and the sleep-steady in and out of Angelica's breathing, the room was perfectly quiet.

Which only made the thoughts marching through his head seem that much louder.

The charges against him were going to be dropped and he'd just had great sex with a warm, beautiful woman who in roughly five months was going to give birth to his child. He ought to be happy. Hell, he ought to be ecstatic.

And he was, he assured himself. It was just…now that the initial euphoria of Cynthia's stunning good news had worn off, that nagging uneasiness was back, clamoring for attention like a persistent itch that had to be scratched.

He tried to tell himself he didn't get it. That he couldn't imagine what the problem was.

But the longer he lay there, the harder it was to lie to himself.

He let out a breath he hadn't known he was holding. And forced himself to face the truth head on. Ever since his arrest, he'd been living in the present only. Sure, he'd gone through the motions of acting as if he believed in the future—beginning to lay out next year's budget at work, making plans for the baby, even getting married—but deep down he hadn't really had any faith that things would work out.

Instead, he'd been taking things one day at time, refusing to look ahead because he was pretty sure he wouldn't like what was in store for him.

But now he was free and clear, with his whole life stretched out before him.

And he couldn't seem to stem a rising tide of panic.

Making matters worse, Angelica thought she was in love with him. And though a selfish part of him felt fiercely gratified that she did, he knew damn well that for her sake it would be best if she were mistaken.

Not that he didn't care about her. He did. More than he'd ever cared about any other woman in his life. What's more, he considered her a friend, and that was a first for him when it came to the opposite sex. But love?

No, he didn't think so. Love just wasn't for him.

That hadn't stopped him from wanting her, however. And in his effort to woo her, to entice her back into his bed, he'd been so charming that she'd gotten the wrong idea about who he was.

But the day was going to come when she'd find out the truth. And when she did, she'd be devastated. For her sake, it would be best if the reality check came now, before things went any further. She had a right to understand the real character—or lack thereof—of the man she'd married. Even if he hated the idea. And even if she was probably going to get hurt in the process. It still had to be better to do it now than later.

Once again, he looked over at her sleeping face.

For a second his heart was gripped by a terrible pain, and he wasn't sure if he could go through with it.

Yet how could he not?

Doing his best not to disturb her, he started to roll to his feet.

"Riley?" she murmured, a soft sound of protest.

"Shh." He grabbed the afghan off the chair and spread it over her. Unable to stop himself, he let his hand linger, just for a moment, on the warm curve of her neck. "Go back to sleep. It's okay."

But it wasn't. And as he pulled on his clothes, picked up his car keys and walked out of the house, he knew it.

Twelve

There was no mistaking the low rumble of the Corvette's engine.

Seated on the long, ice-green sofa in the living room, Angelica looked up from the book she'd been pretending to read and watched through the front window as the silver sports car pulled into the driveway. Her heart slammed painfully against her ribs, but except for a quick glance at her watch, she forced herself to stay where she was.

It was three o'clock. Twenty-two hours almost to the minute since she'd come deliciously awake on the family room floor, reached for Riley and found him gone.

Just thinking about it made her throat feel tight.

As if she'd had an out-of-body experience, she

had a perfect image in her mind of herself, sitting up and hugging the afghan to her naked body, innocently calling out his name.

There'd been no answer because he wasn't there, of course. She just hadn't known it at the time. Still happy and trusting, she'd climbed to her feet and headed for their bedroom, assuming he'd gone to shower. The bedroom had been empty, however, and the bathroom hadn't shown any signs of recent activity, so she'd walked to the French doors and looked out. But the backyard and pool had also appeared deserted.

Perplexed, but not yet feeling any alarm, she'd taken a few minutes to pull on some clothes and made another circuit of the house before finally thinking to check the garage. Incredibly, she'd actually been surprised to see his car was gone.

And still she hadn't panicked. Instead, she'd told herself with more annoyance than distress that he must have gone to visit his brother or parents to discuss what was happening with his case and had simply forgotten to leave her a note.

That fantasy had persisted until the phone rang. She'd snatched it up, fully expecting to hear his voice, prepared to be relieved. Instead it had been Shane, who *had* been at their parents' house and was calling to congratulate his twin on the imminent clearing of his name.

Not about to admit that she didn't have a clue where her husband was, Angelica had made up a story about how Riley had gone to get Chinese take-out and promised Shane she'd have him call when he got back.

Except that he hadn't come back.

Still, it had taken countless hours—during which she'd had to field at least a dozen congratulatory phone calls from various Fortunes—for her to accept that. And to face the idea that he finally must've had time to reflect upon what Mike had done and that was why he'd left.

Sick with regret, wondering if things would've been different if she'd had the courage to share her suspicions about her brother upfront, telling herself she'd do anything if only he'd give her another chance, she'd spent a long, sleepless night. It had been far worse than when Riley had walked out of her life four months ago, because then she'd just thought she was in love with him.

Now she knew. And the idea that she may have lost him for good was tearing her apart.

Outside, the car door opened and Riley climbed out.

His clothes were wrinkled, his hair rumpled, his cheeks shadowed by two days of beard. He looked like hell, he looked totally beautiful and seeing him on his own two feet, hearty and hale, made her feel weak all over.

But not for long. In a demonstration of how unsteady her emotions were, fast on the heels of her relief came a spurt of anger.

How dare he be okay? How dare he break her heart this way and not have to be carried home on a stretcher?

He started toward the house, disappearing from her line of sight as he reached the front entrance. A second later, the front door swung open and he walked inside.

He pulled off his sunglasses and set them on the entry table. Unaware he was being observed, he squeezed his eyes shut and reached up to pinch the bridge of his nose. In that instant he looked utterly desolate and her anger fled as abruptly as it had appeared.

As if sensing her presence, he looked over and saw her. His hand dropped away and his entire demeanor changed. "Hey." The smile he sent her was pure nonchalance.

Needless to say, she didn't smile back. "Where have you been?"

He came down the single step and sauntered toward her. "Out. What are you doing in here?"

She ignored his question. "Out where?"

He gave his trademark shrug. "Just out. I decided to do some celebrating."

With a slight shock, she realized she didn't believe him. True, he looked terrible, but he was now only a few feet away and she didn't smell a hint of either cigarette smoke or alcohol on him. Nor had the look she'd glimpsed on his unguarded face a moment ago been that of a man who'd just spent a wonderful night enjoying fun and games.

Not that it mattered. It wasn't where he'd been but why that concerned her. And her responsibility for it. She took a deep breath. "I'm sorry, Riley. I'm sorrier than you can imagine for what Mike did.

I know now that I should have told you what I suspected sooner, and I hope you can forgive me. But if you can't—if anybody's going to leave, it ought to be me.''

Inexplicably, he stared at her as if she had two heads. ''What are you talking about?''

''You don't have to pretend. I don't blame you for being angry.''

He raised his hand. ''Hold on a minute. You think I left because of what *Mike* did?'' He shook his head. ''Hell, Angelica, give me a little credit. No way would I hold you responsible for your brother's actions. Anymore than I'd expect my brother to be responsible for mine. As for you not saying anything…you told me yesterday that you didn't want to get my hopes up, and I believe you.''

She tried to tell herself that he was just trying to spare her feelings. Still, she couldn't stop the hope flaring to life inside her, gaining strength as she met his silver gaze and saw the conviction there. With a sense of wonder, she realized he really meant what he said.

He wasn't mad at her. He didn't blame her. He understood.

A terrible weight seemed to lift off her shoulders. Yet even as that burden disappeared, it was replaced by an utter sense of bewilderment. ''But if you're not mad, then why did you leave like that?''

His shoulders rose in another careless shrug. ''Because I felt like it. That's the kind of guy I am.''

She stared at him, momentarily rendered speechless by the absurdity of that statement. ''This really isn't about Mike,'' she said finally, still trying to absorb it.

"No."

"It's about you being a—a bad ass?" She felt ridiculous even saying it.

Riley didn't appear to notice. He shifted his weight onto his hip and nodded. "I told you upfront I'd never be a perfect husband. You should have listened."

Implausibly, she was almost tempted to laugh. Mostly from relief, she realized. But there was also a strong sense of disbelief. Surely, he didn't really mean what he was saying? "I'm sorry, Riley, but I just don't believe you."

"What?"

She climbed to her feet. "I don't believe you," she repeated. "I realize we haven't been together long, but I know you. You're not some self-centered, pleasure-seeking, dissolute playboy. You care. About your parents, your job, your house, our baby—me. Or did you think I wouldn't notice all the nice things you've done?"

"You don't understand. I was just being nice to try to get you into bed."

She shook her head. "No. I see the charm, but I also see the substance. The first time I ever saw you, you rescued me from a group of bullies. You were there for me when Mike died. And the second you found out I was pregnant, you insisted we get married. *That's* the man I fell in love with, and nothing you do or say is going to change my mind."

"Then you're deluding yourself, Angelica."

"I don't think so. And you want to know what

else? I think I finally understand why you ran out on me four months ago.''

''And why's that?''

''Because you were afraid. Afraid of what you were feeling. Afraid to take a chance on love for fear you wouldn't measure up.''

''That's baloney.''

She searched his face, and what she saw there was her own defeat. He clearly had no intention of listening, and the brief burst of hope she'd felt only minutes earlier at the discovery that he didn't blame her for Mike vanished. In its place was a despair so all encompassing it was suddenly hard to breathe. ''All right,'' she managed to say. ''If that's the way you want it.'' Biting her lip, suddenly afraid she was going to cry and determined not to, she began to walk toward the entry.

''Where are you going?''

''To pack.''

''What are you talking about?''

She took a steadying breath and turned as she reached the step. ''I can't stay here. Not like this. So I'm leaving.''

Dismay chased across his face, and she felt a rebirth of hope. ''You can't do that,'' he said forcefully. He paused for an instant, then added, ''What about the baby?''

The words were like a knife in her heart. As glad as she was that he cared about their child, just once she needed to come first. ''The baby will be fine. I know you'll take care of us whether we're under your roof or not. That's what you don't understand,

Riley. I trust you to do the right thing. Now all you have to do is trust yourself.''

And with that, she forced herself to walk away.

Well, hell. That hadn't gone the way he'd intended.

Not sure whether he was more alarmed or aggravated, Riley walked over and dropped onto the couch. Absently propping his dusty sandals on the gleaming surface of the coffee table, he tried to decide what had just happened.

What to you think, Fortune? You just told Angelica you didn't care about her and she left.

Yeah, but he hadn't meant it like that, he defended himself automatically. The last thing he'd intended was to drive her away.

But he had anyway.

Outside, sunshine glinted off the Corvette's silver surface.

He scowled, not feeling even a glimmer of pleasure as he considered the sports car's sleek lines. But then, that was no great surprise after what the car had put him through in the last twenty-four hours.

After he'd left yesterday, he'd taken a long drive into the desert to think and wound up way out in the middle of nowhere with a flat tire. Which might not have been so bad if he hadn't lent his cousin Tyler his jack a few weeks ago. And if his cell phone hadn't needed to be recharged.

After a long uncomfortable night, courtesy of his own disjointed thoughts coupled with the temperature in the desert's tendency to drop once the sun went down, he'd had a long hot walk to the highway, where eventually he'd hitched a ride to the nearest service station. Then, after more delays he'd hitched back, jack in hand, more than a little aware that what had been an adventure at seventeen was a major pain in the ass at thirty-two.

As if that wasn't bad enough, he'd even found himself thinking that the time had come to trade in the Corvette for a sporty sedan, something with a real back seat that could safely accommodate a child car seat.

Of course, that had been back when he'd still had a wife and an upcoming child to look out for.

How the hell could Angelica just walk out on him?

Why shouldn't she? You did it to her. Twice, remember?

But that was different, he told his inner voice waspishly. The first time he'd left had been to save her from a bigger hurt in the future. And when it came to the second time, he'd just been trying to make her realize that he couldn't be trusted so he wouldn't disappoint her later.

The latter thought froze him in place. It had seemed perfectly logical yesterday. But now...

Now it sounded sort of lame. Like a man grasping at straws. Like a man who was afraid to admit he was in love. Like a man who, just the way Angelica had said, couldn't face the prospect of not measuring up.

And even so, all the way along, she'd believed in him, he realized. She'd had faith in his innocence with no proof but her own intuition. She'd trusted that he'd take care of her enough to marry him. She'd risked her heart to make love with him. And even though it must've been painful, she'd been willing to go through her brother's things to try and clear his name.

For the first time it occurred to him how much it must've hurt her to face what Mike had done. Yet she'd never said a word. Instead, she'd celebrated his own good fortune with all her heart.

With a groan at his blind self-centeredness, he shoved an errant lock of hair off his forehead and let his head fall back against the couch cushion.

And still the thoughts kept coming.

He found himself remembering the night at the carnival, and what Angelica had said when he'd talked about being a disappointment to his parents. *"Yes, but that was a long time ago. You're an adult now."*

She was right, of course. The irony was, that in all the ways that mattered, he'd put his bad boy persona behind him some time ago, living a fairly respectable life—until the first time he'd slept with her. Overwhelmed by the power of his feelings, he'd panicked and taken off. And then, before he could get things in perspective, his arrest had come. Irrational as he knew it was now, he realized that on some level he'd believed he'd brought it on himself, due to his boyhood reputation—and his recent, irresponsible actions.

But loving Angelica had changed all that, he thought now. Time and again she'd demonstrated her faith in him, a faith he wanted to live up to. Just as he wanted a chance to show her that her love wasn't misplaced.

Yet he'd let her down. Again.

But she wasn't gone yet.

He climbed to his feet. He had to talk to her, and he just prayed it wasn't too late.

Angelica stood at the terrace rail, the harsh afternoon sun beating down on her head. She knew she should go inside and gather her belongings, but she needed some time first to pull herself together. She was just so...cold.

She watched the sunlight dance on the brilliant blue surface of the pool. Heaven help her but she didn't want to go. And not, she thought, looking around, because this beautiful place had begun to feel like home.

But because she didn't want to leave Riley.

Except that Riley had made it very clear that he didn't love her—and probably never would. The misery inside her increased.

"Angelica?" For a moment she thought she was imagining his voice. But then he stepped up beside her, tall and real and solid.

She stiffened. "I was just going—

"Don't." He touched his hand to her shoulder, freezing her in place. "Please."

The entreaty in his voice startled her. Before she could stop herself, she glanced up at him.

To her shock, he was looking back at her intently. Meeting her gaze, he swallowed almost as if he were nervous, and then a faint, self-deprecating smile curved across his sensual mouth. "I'm glad you're still here. I looked for you in the bedroom, and when I couldn't find you I was afraid that while I was sitting on my butt in the living room being nine kinds of fool, you'd left.''

She couldn't think how to answer that so she just continued to stare at him.

"The thing is—'' He stopped and shoved a hand through his hair as if not certain how to continue. "Aw, hell, Angel, I love you. It's just taken me awhile to figure it out."

The sun must finally be getting to her, she thought desperately. She dampened her suddenly dry lips. "What?''

"I love you. And you were right when you accused me of panicking that first time we made love. I'd never felt like that before, with anyone, and it scared the hell out of me. But I love you so much, Angelica. And I'm a better man when you're around. Stay."

To her chagrin, the tears she'd refused to shed suddenly welled up in her eyes and spilled over. "Oh, Riley.''

Stricken, he said desperately, "Please, baby. Please don't cry.''

"I'm just so happy," she said, smiling even though the tears refused to stop.

Clearly not knowing what else to do, he pulled her into his arms and kissed her.

And that's when she finally knew for sure that it was all going to be all right.

Epilogue

Two days later

"**I** can't believe we're late." Tucking a wayward strand of hair behind her ear, Angelica glanced reproachfully at Riley as they hurried toward the church.

"Hey, don't look at me that way," he protested without any heat. "You were the one who insisted on wandering around the house in that sexy lingerie. I just reacted like any red-blooded man who's madly in love with his wife."

"I wasn't 'wandering around.'" Her attempt to sound severe was ruined by the warm glow in her eyes as she looked at him. "I was in the process of getting dressed for this wedding and you ambushed me."

"Funny," he said mildly as they reached the church's massive front doors. "I don't remember you protesting."

"That's because you were too busy ravishing me," she shot back in the prim tone that never failed to amuse him.

He started to pull the doors open, then thought better of it. Letting go, he leaned over, pressed a tender kiss to the corner of her mouth and murmured, "I'm not sorry for it, either."

Her eyes filled with a mixture of humor and tenderness. "Me neither." Angling her head, she leaned into him and captured his lips with her own.

They were immediately lost in each other, oblivious to the hoot of an appreciative passerby, the sweetness of the kiss the only thing that mattered. They were both more than a little out of breath when they finally came up for air. "See." Riley couldn't resist one more quick buss to her mouth. "You do find me irresistible."

"You're incorrigible." She shook her head in mock despair and then her eyes suddenly widened. "Oh my gosh!"

"What is it? What's the matter?"

"I think—I think I just felt the baby move."

"You're kidding." He instantly reached out and pressed his hand against the slight curve of her abdomen. "Where?" Stymied when he felt nothing, he shifted his fingers and was rewarded by the faintest quiver, like butterfly wings tickling his palm. He looked up in wonder. "I think I felt it."

They stared at each other, grinning like fools, until Angelica suddenly seemed to remember where they were. "Don't you think we'd better go in? Isabelle will never forgive us if we miss her big day entirely."

"Right." Still feeling awed, he pulled open the door and they walked inside, instantly enveloped in the sweet scent of flowers.

"Well, it's about time." Resplendent in an elegant gray cutaway, Riley's father Hunter stood in the vestibule, next to Riley's mother. "We were starting to think you two weren't going to show up."

"Sorry, Dad. We got hung up."

Although the elder Fortune's face remained grave, his dark eyes warmed as he looked from his son to his new daughter-in-law, who he'd finally met the previous night at the rehearsal dinner. "I suppose that's understandable," he said gallantly. "Angelica, you look beautiful."

Angelica flushed with pleased surprise. "Thank you."

Riley felt a tug of tenderness, knowing she still couldn't quite believe that rather than the disapproval at Mike's actions that she'd expected, his family was extremely grateful to her for clearing him instead. "How's Isabelle holding up?" he asked his mother.

Joan glanced at her watch, appearing distracted. "She's all right. Maybe a little quiet, but I suppose that's to be expected." She straightened, suddenly looking like her usual efficient self as one of the ushers approached at the same time that the bridesmaids piled out of the sanctuary. She looked up at

Riley. "You and Angelica had better go sit down now, so I can be seated and we can get started."

"Right. I'll see you inside," he said, settling his hand on the small of his wife's back and urging her toward the aisle. "Are you sorry we didn't have a big church wedding?" he asked, ignoring the stares they were provoking with their late arrival.

She gave his hand a squeeze. "Not at all. But this is certainly beautiful. Your mother outdid herself."

That much was true. The church looked exquisite. Elegant sprays of pale pink lilies tied with cascading white satin bows decorated the end of each burnished mahogany pew. The altar was awash in more of the flawless flowers, while dozens of white candles glowed beneath the rosy light from the stained-glass windows. An organ played in the upper balcony, the perfect foil for the soft murmuring of the nearly one thousand guests packed into the place.

Approaching the family area at the front of the church, he nodded as his eye caught that of Julie Fortune, sitting close to his cousin Tyler, who was now her husband. On the other side of Tyler sat his other cousin Jason, also a partner in Fortune Construction, whose usually serious face seemed to light up as he watched his six-year-old daughter Lisa say something to his bride, Adele, that brought a smile to both females faces.

Stopping at the pew in front of his cousins and their wives, he waited as Shane, Cynthia and their son, Bobby, looking too damn cute for words in a dark suit that was a miniature of his father's, slid over to make room as he and Angelica joined them.

"We'd about given up on you," Shane informed him.

"Relax," he told his twin. "I already heard the same thing from Dad."

"Did you get a chance to see Isabelle?"

He shook his head, and they both fell silent as their mother appeared on the arm of an usher and sat down next to regal Kate Fortune in the row in front of them.

A minute passed, and then the door on one side of the altar opened and the groom and his men walked out and took up their positions. A moment after that, the bridesmaids started down the aisle.

When they were finally in place, the organist struck up the wedding march.

Like everyone else in the church, Riley got to his feet and turned to look up the aisle, expecting to see Isabelle make her grand entrance.

But instead of an exquisite bride in a billowing white dress on the arm of her proud father, the aisle was empty.

A faint buzz went through the gathered throng. It slowly grew in strength, only to instantly die down as Riley's father suddenly appeared, ominously alone. The strain on his face obvious, Hunter Fortune signaled peremptorily to the organist to quit playing.

In the ensuing silence, his voice rang out. "I'm sorry. I'm afraid the ceremony will have to be postponed. My daughter—" for the briefest instant his iron composure seemed to waiver and then he steadied himself "—Isabelle appears to be missing."

A disbelieving murmur ran through the church. The sound grew progressively louder as the groom made a choked cry of protest and bolted up the aisle himself.

"I don't believe this," Shane murmured as the church rapidly began to empty as people surged up the aisles, clearly hoping to learn more about the unfolding drama.

"Believe it," Riley shot back.

"Nothing's ever dull with the Fortunes," Tyler murmured from behind them.

Truer words had never been spoken, Riley thought as he leaned forward and laid a hand on his mother's shoulder. "Are you all right, Mom?"

"No, I'm not," Joan said, climbing to her feet. "Obviously I need to talk to your father." Without another word, she headed toward the vestibule.

"I guess we'd better go, too," Shane said, directing Cynthia and Bobby toward the outside aisle. "Mom and Dad will need our support.

Angelica made as if to follow, but Riley restrained her with a touch to her shoulder. "Hold on a minute."

"What?"

Taking her hand, he lead her into the main aisle and toward the altar. Stopping before the candles and the banks of flowers, he said quietly, "I just want you to know you're the best thing that ever happened to me. I love you, Angel."

Angelica looked up into his handsome, beloved face, her heart filled with wonder at the words even though it was hardly the first time she'd heard them in the past few days. She swallowed. "I love you, too."

"I know you do, baby, and I thank God for it every day." And with that he bent down and kissed her with everything in his heart.

Finally, he straightened. "Now," he said huskily, "let's go see if we can find out what's going on with my sister."

Hand in hand, together at last, they started up the aisle.

* * * * *

*Find out what happens when
Isabelle Fortune runs from her
wedding and right into the arms
of her right groom*

in

GROOM OF FORTUNE,

*coming only to Silhouette Desire
in December 2000.*

*For a sneak preview, please
turn the page.*

One

How would Isabelle Fortune take the news when he told her that the man she loved was a murderer?

She'd hate him. Link Templeton had had enough experience handing out bad news in his job as a criminal investigator for the city of Pueblo to know that the messenger rarely received any praise from the family and friends of the accused. Hadn't he already felt the sting of the Fortune's outrage when he'd been forced to arrest Riley Fortune, Isabelle's brother, as a suspect in the death of Mike Dodd?

He growled low in his throat, glaring at the road ahead. It didn't matter what Isabelle Fortune *or* her family thought of him. It was the case that was important. It was slapping iron on a guilty man's wrists and jerking another criminal off the streets that brought him satisfaction. It was a job.

But stopping a society wedding wasn't.

He slapped an angry palm against the steering wheel. But he couldn't just stand by and permit Isabelle to marry Brad Rowan. Not when he knew the man was capable of murder. What if, after their marriage, Isabelle happened upon some bit of information that pointed to Brad's guilt? Would Brad kill her, too, as he had Mike, to silence her? The very thought had Link curling his fingers tighter around the steering wheel. He wouldn't let Brad harm her. He couldn't. He—

Link shoved the unwanted thoughts aside, but try as he might, he couldn't erase the image of Isabelle the thoughts had drawn. He remembered the day when he'd accidentally stumbled into a wedding shower held in Isabelle's honor. When his gaze had met Isabelle's, it was as if lightning had struck. He'd stood immobile, paralyzed by the violet eyes that had met his, his pulse pounding in his ears, every nerve in his body burning with awareness.

And he was sure that she'd been similarly affected. A laugh from a guest was what had finally shocked him into movement. He'd torn his gaze from hers and turned away...but he'd never forgotten the look in her eyes. The awareness. The desire. He'd recognized them, because he'd lived with both ever since that day.

He snorted in disgust. She's in love with another

man, he reminded himself. And even if she wasn't, he was too old and too jaded to make a play for a woman like her.

Link caught a flash of red in the church parking lot ahead, then a convertible sports car shot out of the lot and directly into his path. "Damn!" He stomped on the brake, whipping the steering wheel to the right to avoid broadsiding the small foreign car.

His heart pumping like a jackhammer, he stared after the car, watching as the woman behind the wheel ripped a wedding veil from her head and held it up, letting the wind have it. The delicate lace panels sailed behind her for a moment, then floated slowly to the street, like a kite with a broken string.

Isabelle? he asked himself, recognizing the pricey foreign car and its driver. Where was she going? She was supposed to be getting married. What the hell had happened?

He glanced toward the church for an answer, but the thick entry doors were closed. And though the parking lot was full, there wasn't a soul in sight. He glanced in the direction of the red sports car, then back to the church where the wedding was to have taken place. *It's none of your business,* he told himself. *You've got no jurisdiction when it comes to Isabelle Fortune's personal affairs.*

"Like hell, I don't," he muttered. Setting his jaw,

he turned his face to the street ahead, stomped on the clutch and shifted into first. Peeling out and leaving a trail of black rubber in his wake, he took off in the direction the red sports car had taken.

FORTUNE FAMILY TREE: THE ARIZONA BRANCH

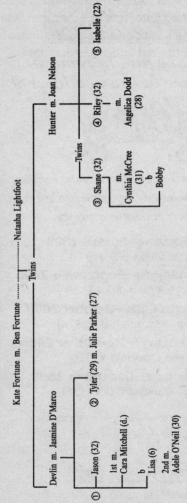

Kate Fortune m. Ben Fortune ·········· Natasha Lightfoot

Twins

Devlin m. Jasmine D'Marco

② Tyler (29) m. Julie Parker (27)

Hunter m. Joan Nelson

① Jason (32)

1st m. Cara Mitchell (d.)

b
Lisa (6)

2nd m. Adele O'Neil (30)

Twins

③ Shane (32)
m.
Cynthia McCree (31)
b
Bobby

④ Riley (32)
m.
Angelica Dodd (28)

⑤ Isabelle (22)

d. deceased
····· affair

① Bride of Fortune
② Mail-Order Cinderella
③ Fortune's Secret Child
④ Husband——or Enemy?
⑤ Groom of Fortune

You're not going to believe this offer!

In October and November 2000, buy any two Harlequin or Silhouette books and save $10.00 off future purchases, or buy any three and save $20.00 off future purchases!

Just fill out this form and attach 2 proofs of purchase (cash register receipts) from October and November 2000 books and Harlequin will send you a coupon booklet worth a total savings of $10.00 off future purchases of Harlequin and Silhouette books in 2001. Send us 3 proofs of purchase and we will send you a coupon booklet worth a total savings of $20.00 off future purchases.

Saving money has never been this easy.

I accept your offer! Please send me a coupon booklet:

Name: _____

Address: _____ City: _____

State/Prov.: _____ Zip/Postal Code: _____

Optional Survey!

In a typical month, how many Harlequin or Silhouette books would you buy <u>new</u> at retail stores?

☐ Less than 1   ☐ 1   ☐ 2   ☐ 3 to 4   ☐ 5+

Which of the following statements best describes how you <u>buy</u> Harlequin or Silhouette books? Choose one answer only that <u>best</u> describes you.

☐ I am a regular buyer and reader

☐ I am a regular reader but buy only occasionally

☐ I only buy and read for specific times of the year, e.g. vacations

☐ I subscribe through Reader Service but also buy at retail stores

☐ I mainly borrow and buy only occasionally

☐ I am an occasional buyer and reader

Which of the following statements best describes how you <u>choose</u> the Harlequin and Silhouette series books you buy <u>new</u> at retail stores? By "series," we mean books within a particular line, such as *Harlequin PRESENTS* or *Silhouette SPECIAL EDITION*. Choose one answer only that <u>best</u> describes you.

☐ I only buy books from my favorite series

☐ I generally buy books from my favorite series but also buy books from other series on occasion

☐ I buy some books from my favorite series but also buy from many other series regularly

☐ I buy all types of books depending on my mood and what I find interesting and have no favorite series

Please send this form, along with your cash register receipts as proofs of purchase, to:

In the U.S.: Harlequin Books, P.O. Box 9057, Buffalo, NY 14269

In Canada: Harlequin Books, P.O. Box 622, Fort Erie, Ontario L2A 5X3

(Allow 4-6 weeks for delivery) Offer expires December 31, 2000.   PHQ4002

If you enjoyed what you just read,
then we've got an offer you can't resist!

Take 2 bestselling love stories FREE!
Plus get a FREE surprise gift!

July 2000
BACHELOR DOCTOR
#1303 by Barbara Boswell

August 2000
THE RETURN OF ADAMS CADE
#1309 by BJ James
Men of Belle Terre

September 2000
SLOW WALTZ ACROSS TEXAS
#1315 by Peggy Moreland
Texas Grooms

October 2000
THE DAKOTA MAN
#1321 by Joan Hohl

November 2000
HER PERFECT MAN
#1328 by Mary Lynn Baxter

December 2000
IRRESISTIBLE YOU
#1333 by Barbara Boswell

MAN OF THE MONTH

For twenty years Silhouette has been giving you the ultimate in romantic reads. Come join some of your favorite authors in helping us to celebrate our anniversary with the most rugged, sexy and lovable heroes ever!

Available at your favorite retail outlet.

Silhouette®
Where love comes alive™